Little Bronze Girl

Hettie Aston

Published by Hettie Aston
Publishing partner: Paragon Publishing, Rothersthorpe
First published 2020

ISBN 978-1-78222-781-6

Book design, layout and production management by Into Print
www.intoprint.net
+44 (0)1604 832149

Dedicated to

All Nurses Past and Present
Care given with patience, skill and humour
even in the most difficult of times

Little Bronze Girl

One

In **May 1933** Iona House was visited by a guest, both uninvited and unwelcome. She crept in, unnoticed at first, but the effect of her visit caused havoc. The name of this visitor was Bordettella Pertusis. (Whooping Cough)

The arrival of this disease in our home was not totally unexpected as Dr Salmanowicz, our family doctor, had told us of cases in the town; also several children at John and Alfie's school were ill with the infection. As a precaution we had been advised to isolate baby Rory and Claudette for their safety.

My young half-brothers, John almost 9 and Alfie now 6 years old, and I had been living with our aunt Vera and uncle Angus in their beautiful Gothic style, Victorian house in the North East of England iron and steel town of Ransington since the death of our mother, over a year before. Our 17 month old baby sister, Claudette, had now been officially adopted by Vera and Angus as, prior to our arrival, they were childless and had always longed for a baby. Unexpectedly Vera then gave birth to Rory in September 1932.

Fortunately Iona House was a large seven bedroomed property with extensive gardens, overlooking the park, so there was plenty of room for us all.

The boys became sick first with, what appeared to be a sore throat and head cold, quickly changing into a choking, whooping cough, so bad at times they could hardly breathe. Claudette also developed the infection so her cot was moved into the boy's bedroom to make nursing three poorly children easier.

My aunt Vera kept baby Rory well away from the sick room; breast feeding him in her bedroom and taking him downstairs with her whilst she made fresh juice and puréed vegetables; produce from the garden, brought in by Mr Handyside the gardener.

He was forcing some strawberries in the heated greenhouse which he thought might tempt the children to eat.

John, Alfie and Claudette coughed and choked on their mucous, it was pitiful to witness all three children sweating and vomiting as they attempted to gasp air into their lungs. The serious nature of the illness and the high mortality rate which accompanied it prompted Vera and Angus to make the decision to contact the boys' father, our mother's widower, Herbert Flitch.

Great aunt Eliza Jane, who lived in Newcastle upon Tyne, being the person most likely to know of Herbert's whereabouts was asked, by telephone, to try to make contact and notify him about his sick children. Herbert Flitch had been my mother's second husband up until her death in September 1931. My own father, Alfred Dawson, died a few months after he was demobbed from the army after serving in the Great War.

Daytime care of John, Alfie and Claudette was shared between myself and Bonny, our mothers help. Night nurse Fellows took over at 9pm when I left the children in her capable hands.

Jean Fellows, newly retired from hospital nursing as she

had recently married, came personally recommended by Dr Salmanowicz; she was calm, cheerful and experienced. This meant I could have a few hours much needed sleep. She brought a Wrights Coal Tar infuser with her which burnt throughout each night. The sprigs of rosemary placed around the room, which Jean acknowledged was an old fashioned remedy, she felt helped with breathing. Other than that she said it was just a question of nursing the children and persuading them to eat small amounts of nourishing food and drink plenty, whilst waiting for the illness to run its course.

A syrup of hyssop and rosemary was administered four times daily to our patients and twice each day their chests and backs were rubbed with camphorated oil and eucalyptus. Sometimes we would sit with them in a steam filled bathroom to aid their breathing.

One afternoon Bonny answered the front door to Herbert Flitch and his mother, Mrs Lucrettia Flitch, who immediately demanded to know where her grandsons were and who was looking after them. Adding that she hoped they were being cared for properly; a complete irony as she and her son had chosen to abandon the boys.

On arrival at the bedroom where I was about to give medicine to the children Mrs Flitch rasped at me, "Oh I might have known you'd be calling the shots Betty Dawson. Think yourself Florence Nightingale now I suppose." (I hated being called Betty)

I did not respond but continued to give the children their syrup and juice.

Mrs Flitch looked at the bottle of syrup and commented in a loud voice, as she made herself comfortable in the armchair, "If you think that's going to do any good you've got another think coming. Most kids die of the whooping cough – it's a well known fact."

Herbert said nothing. Hovering like a large feeble moth he just stared at his boys and they stared back as if he was a stranger.

Claudette began to cough and choke, I immediately went to her. Holding a vomit bowl whilst she attempted to expectorate the thick, sticky mucous from her throat and chest. Her bloodshot eyes watered with the effort and I could see she was becoming exhausted. Bordetella Pertusis was beginning to take its toll!

When I turned from the child Mrs Flitch had left the room. I must have looked puzzled.

Herbert's explanation was, "She's gone to the toilet."

On her return, some 15 minutes later Mrs Flitch announced, "That's it then, we are going, come on Herby."

With that they left.

Later, when I went to my bedroom I could tell my things had been disturbed.

The top drawer of my knee hole dressing table was slightly open and my underwear drawer was not as I had left it. My parents, Louisa and Alfred's, wedding picture had fallen over and my money had gone from the little china dish beside my hairbrush. Lucrettia Flitch had violated my privacy, stolen from me and I was furious with her. However I felt secure in the knowledge that the thing she had been searching for, my dad's war medal, was safely hidden where she would never find it.

Either Dr Salmanowicz or Dr Anna, his fiancé, visited the children most days and gradually the coughing subsided and their energy returned. Bonny or I would read them stories or play for a short time, but the most important thing now was to persuade them to eat some of the delicious soups, jellies and custards which Vera had made. It was difficult at first but gradually, as their appetites improved, they ate more, especially the strawberries, and began to recover.

A knock on the bedroom door one day heralded a visit from Stan, my boyfriend, whom all three children adored but especially John and Alfie. They chatted about football and Stan promised them a game in the park as soon as they were well enough, perhaps followed by ice cream.

"Me swell , me swell ," shouted Claudette.

"Yes, you too," I said. We were all smiling for the first time in weeks.

2

The Train Journey

It took about a month for Bordettella Pertusis to depart Iona House. Thankfully all three affected children survived.

Claudette was happy to be reunited with her mother Vera and baby brother Rory. She gradually returned to being a busy, happy toddler.

John and Alfie returned to school but found the morning and afternoon walk tiring. I suggested to Stan that I might use his bicycle with the box cart fitted to the back as transport for them, to which he readily agreed.

I adapted a skirt into culottes which I thought would make for a more elegant mount and dismount from the bicycle. Each day the journey to and from school was accomplished with one boy in the cart and the other on the cross bar, onto which Percy, our chauffeur-handyman had fixed a small seat.

My sewing had been abandoned whilst the children were ill. I had missed both the sewing and spending time in my beautiful circular room in the tower of the house, from where the view over the town was spectacular. Plans for making another quilt had had to be put on hold. My sewing room was also the office for Stan's tree and gardening business where I worked; keeping the accounts straight and indexing his work schedule. This had also fallen behind, but now John and Alfie were back at school I knew I would soon catch up.

"How would you like a night out at the pictures?" Stan asked.

"That I would like," I said, "but only if we can see 'Footlight Parade' with James Cagney." I'd heard it was on at the Roxy.

"King Kong is on in a couple of weeks," Stan said. "That's more my style, but if you want 'Footlight Parade' then 'Footlight Parade' it is."

Sitting with Stan together in a double seat on the back row at the pictures I was aware that other couples were kissing, becoming more and more amorous and did not actually show any interest in the film at all. The usherette shone her torch on one couple and said, "Pack it in. If I have to tell you two again, you'll be thrown out."

I could tell that she meant it so hand-holding and the occasional kiss was as amorous as I would allow.

The Pathe News always held interest for me and I already knew that Adolf Hitler was now the German Chancellor. He seemed to have enormous popularity in Germany, holding rallies and stirring the people into following him.

A letter arrived for me in June the contents of which made my heart leap. It was from my great aunt Eliza Jane, who was my late grandmother's sister.

High Stones,
Gosforth.

14th June, 1933.

My Dear Bettina,

Vera has been updating me regarding the whooping cough situation at Iona House. I am delighted to hear that all three children have recovered and that baby Rory did not contract the disease.

I understand that you have been more or less housebound for over a month now and wonder if you would care to come and stay here with me for a little holiday.

Your loving aunt,
Eliza Jane.

The idea of a holiday was exciting, never having had one before, but I was unsure how I would accomplish it. I decided to talk it over with my aunt Vera then try to formulate a plan.

"A holiday, what a brilliant idea," Vera said.

"I know," I agreed, "but I'm not sure how I can organise the boys and the office."

'Perhaps Bonny would work some extra hours,' I thought.

Bonny agreed and would be happy to work extra hours picking John and Alfie up at the end of their school day but on one condition. That was for me to make her a pair of culottes so that she could use the bicycle with the box cart and retain her modesty.

Stan's business had grown since he started it about a year ago. His expertise was in trimming and felling trees. The owners of the trees were happy to pay Stan a good rate because they knew he was excellent at his job and would take care around their property. Angus's brother, Ian McLeod, was Stan's silent business partner making an initial investment of £150 to enable Stan to buy essential equipment and a second-hand van. Apart from expenses of fuel for the van and chain saw there were no other costs as Vera and Angus provided the office in the tower room rent free. After a few months Stan was able to pay me a wage of £2 for about 10 hours work each week which I considered to be fair.

When Stan called into the office I told him about the holiday and asked him, "Would you be willing to take the boys to school in the van each morning to help whilst I'm away?"

"Of course I would," he replied. "You deserve a holiday and I will help where I can."

I discussed the office work with him and it was agreed that I would bank the cash before I went and leave the books all up to date, Stan's work schedule would be on the desk for him; then I'd pick up where I left off on my return.

I wrote to great aunt Eliza Jane confirming that I would be delighted to visit her and a date was arranged for the end of June.

John and Alfie promised to be ready for Stan by 8:30 am each morning and be good for Vera and Bonny. I felt bad leaving them but I knew they would be well looked after and I was so much looking forward to seeing Eliza Jane again.

The train journey was pleasant and uneventful allowing me the luxury of reading a magazine and completing two crosswords. Passengers entered and left the carriage compartment at the various stations; most of them unremarkable.

The exception being one large lady who, as we were the only two passengers in the carriage at the time, produced a bottle of water, soap, flannel and a small towel then proceeded to wash and dry under her arms. She then fully exposed each of her breasts, washed and dried them thoroughly, finishing with a liberal dusting of talcum powder. She seemed blissfully unaware of my presence and I kept my head in my magazine, with unavoidable observation being from the corner of my eye.

Six down, three across, became difficult to concentrate on as she pulled up her skirt to wash between her legs.

"Cooze wash, cooze wash," she repeated to herself. "Cooze dry, cooze dry." Then a cloud of talcum powder which, drifting my way, brought with it the scent of lily of the valley.

She alighted from the train one stop before me to be greeted on the platform with a kiss from a man, I fancifully thought he may be her lover whom I hoped would appreciate the effort she had made to smell sweet for him.

After reading an article in the newspaper regarding the dangers women face when travelling alone I had taken the precaution of wearing a long hat pin; to be used in self defence should it be required.

Two young men, smelling of drink, entered the carriage after the lady left. One sat beside me and the other one sat opposite, crowding me. They persisted on leaning into me and making lecherous comments; there was no corridor into which I could escape. Fortunately it was only a short journey to my station.

I knew I would have to reach for my suitcase in the overhead rack and, sensing I might have some difficulty with them, I had removed the hat pin and concealed it up my sleeve.

They were both laughing and touching me as I collected my things together and one stood over me, pushing his face into mine as the train pulled into the station.

Trying not to inhale his foetid breath I addressed him, in

what I hoped was an authoritative tone, whilst pointing the seven inch steel hat pin in his direction,

"My uncle is meeting me off this train. He is in the constabulary and I'm sure would enjoy a word with you and your apology of a friend over there. Touch me again and you'll get this, right in you. So back off you couple of pathetic bastards."

I had the steel hat pin pointing at his crotch.

Much to my surprise they did back off and I alighted from the train unscathed.

I was to be met at the Central Station, Newcastle-upon-Tyne by my cousins Winnie and Gladys. We had not met before so they would be holding a large piece of card with my name on it for ease of identification. Sure enough they were waiting for me with my name, BETTINA, written in bold capitals. Even without the name I would have known it was them. Winnie and Gladys each had brought their husbands, Cedric and Cyril who were, confusingly, identical twins. All four of them worked in the family business *Gibbs Funeral Care*; all were dressed, top to toe, in black and wearing solemn expressions, which I considered must be a necessity of the job. I did wonder briefly if Winnie and Gladys ever mixed their husbands up!

The moment I said, "Hello, I'm Bettina" they all smiled and hugged me making it a truly memorable, if slightly bizarre, meeting.

A short car journey took us to High Stones which was the home they all shared with aunt Eliza Jane who was the company director of their funeral business, *Gibbs Funeral Care*.

High Stones was an impressively large, white, Art Deco style building, having a flat roof and black, metal curved window frames. This recently built, opulent, modern property with clean lines and an indoor, heated swimming pool screamed 'no expense spared' at me.

Great aunt Eliza Jane made me feel welcome, her hug was reassuringly warm and I just had the feeling that my holiday was going to be wonderful.

3

The Holiday

"**Oh Bettina pet**, I've really missed you, I'm so glad you are here," aunt Eliza Jane said. "Now let's have a cup of tea and a slice of my orange cake, which I know is your favourite, and we can discuss the itinerary."

Eliza Jane, an excellent cook, was correct, her orange cake was my favourite. At age 77 years she still cooked for all her family as, I was given to understand, neither Winnie nor Gladys enjoyed being in the kitchen; both preferring to focus on the business of running *Gibbs Funeral Care*.

"Now I need to know, do you want to go to the coast, the country, the city for shopping, or all of the above?" she asked in a palpably excited tone. "The swimming pool is there for you to use when ever you want, can you swim Bettina?"

This was something we had never discussed before but I assured her that, although I was not a strong swimmer, I could swim and would have been looking forward to going in the pool but, unfortunately I hadn't brought a swimming costume.

"That settles it then," she said. "We are going shopping this afternoon and we'll have you rigged out fit for the Olympics."

I was to be staying at High Stones for five days so, following our conversation I was anticipating having a lovely time.

Eliza Jane showed me to my room with its curved, Crittall, bay windows and adjoining bathroom which had green and black glass tiles on the walls and floor and a shower imported from America. The house had been architect designed especially for her and she loved the clean lines and minimalist features. The swimming pool was most impressive; the thought of plunging into the crystal clear water caused my toes to tingle with pleasure.

Fenwicks, a huge department store in Newcastle, appeared to sell everything anyone could wish for. It is where I chose a swimming costume in blue with a matching swimming cap. My aunt insisted on paying for them, then announced we would now be going to Bainbridges as they had a well stocked fabric and haberdashery department.

The display of fabric bolts was the biggest and best I'd ever seen and I purchased several yards of pretty floral cotton which would make a day dress and some tweed to make into trousers for myself, as I imagined I would be cycling with the boys to school this winter.

"Well I reckon we deserve a cup of coffee now," aunt Eliza Jane announced, "we'll go to Pumphries."

Leaving the shop we made our way down towards the Cloth Market. "Pumphries sells the best coffee in town," Eliza Jane assured me.

Who should be playing his barrel organ on a street corner but Geordie Brown, looking his usual dapper self in a bright red waistcoat and bowler hat but without Tink his monkey.

"I know him," I said. "That's Geordie Brown from Durham. "He sometimes has a pitch beside the fisher women in Ransington. He wants to marry one of them."

"Geordie Brown from Durham, my eye," Eliza Jane said. "He's Sonny Thompson from Sunderland and what's more has a girl in every port. Steer clear of him pet."

"I wonder where his monkey is?" I asked.

"Last I heard, he'd put it in a zoo," was her reply as we continued walking.

Passing through the ground floor of Pumphries the pungent aroma of roasting coffee and the sound of the beans being ground would delight all coffee lovers, including myself. Upstairs was the coffee shop with string racks above the seats on which gentlemen placed their hats. This reminded me of the railway carriage which had similar storage for hats, parcels or small bags.

We discussed the Flitches and I told my aunt about their visit to Iona House and how I was sure Mrs Flitch had been through my personal things and stolen some money.

"That's Lucrettia Flitch all over, she'll never change, disgrace of a woman she is.

What's even more worrying that son of hers now has a stall on the quayside at the Sunday market. He's up to no good, I'm sure of it. I bet you a pound to a penny the stuff he's selling is knocked off," aunt said.

This was said with such conviction I was inclined to believe her.

"Time for home," Eliza said, as we walked down a side street and into an office which I quickly realised was *Gibbs Funeral Care*. I was introduced to several members of staff, all wearing black but with remarkably cheery smiles, before entering a courtyard containing three hearses and several big black Humber limousines.

"Adam here will be chauffeuring us for the week and we have the use of this limousine, unless it's required for a funeral of course," aunt said.

We climbed in and Adam, whom I hadn't failed to notice

was a good looking young man with dark brown wavy hair of around 20 years at a guess, drove us home in style.

Each day there was a new place to visit and usually we had lunch or coffee by the sea or in the country.

One day Adam stopped the car outside a handsome four storey town house in Newcastle-upon-Tyne.

"This is the house where your mother, Louisa, and your aunt Vera were born, and where your grandmother, Letticia Ann started her bed and breakfast after she was widowed" Eliza Jane said. "It is still a bed and breakfast establishment. I know the lady who runs it, would you like to go in?"

I nodded in reply and we climbed the steps and aunt knocked on the door.

Mrs Freda Tolson welcomed us in and I had the impression that our visit was not unexpected.

"I've made teacakes Eliza, to have with a cuppa," said Mrs Tolson who then asked. "Would you and your niece like to have a look around?"

"I'm sure she would. Adam won't be back until 4 o'clock so no hurry. I'll just sit here and watch the world go by Freda," aunt replied, settling into a chair beside the net curtained window.

I followed Mrs Tolson around all the floors of the house.

"I believe this was the original sitting room," Mrs Tolson said, as we went into a large, first floor square room which had a high, imposing plaster ceiling rose and a frieze of plaster grapes.

I was shown the largest bedroom where, Mrs Tolson informed me, "this was probably the room where your mother Louisa and your aunt Vera were born."

The attic rooms, I was told, would have been for the servants. Two now comfortably furnished as bedrooms and the third converted into a bathroom.

Outside I was shown what used to be the stables with accommodation for the groom above. All now used for storage.

"Have you been running the bed and breakfast long?" I asked Mrs Tolson.

"Only a year," she replied. "It was in a shabby state when we took it on. My husband is very handy though and we more or less gutted the place before we opened."

"It certainly is a beautiful house," I said. "Do you know when it was built?"

"Around 1760 I think. I'm told it's Georgian. The whole terrace is Georgian," she replied.

"I'm finding it amazing to be standing in the room where my mother and aunt Vera were born," I said as we re-entered the main bedroom.

Mrs Tolson then opened the door of a huge walk-in cupboard and went in.

"I'm just looking for my torch," she said. "I need to get Mr Tolson to put an electric light in here. It's like being down the pit."

I wasn't sure if I was meant to follow so I just stood at the cupboard entrance.

Mrs Tolson had disappeared but I could see the beam of her torch and heard a lot of banging, crashing and one or two swear words.

"Found it," she shouted.

Finally she emerged struggling to carry a huge oil painting in a gold frame. It was in need of a good clean but I could see it was of a young woman and two small girls.

"I've been meaning to give this to Eliza for ages," said Mrs Tolson, dusting herself down.

"What a lovely picture, don't you want to keep it?" I said.

"Oh no, it's not mine Bettina. It belongs to your aunt as does this house. We only run the bed and breakfast for her."

"Oh I hadn't realised," I said.

"Yes. I used to work at Gibbs Funeral Care then this property came up for sale as a going concern. My husband was out of work so Eliza bought it and asked us to run the place for her."

"What a lovely idea," I said. "Keeping Letticia Ann's house in the family."

"I know. Eliza's kindness itself, been very good to us she has. Mind you nothing much gets past her in business, good business woman she is."

"This house must hold lots of secrets; being so old," I remarked.

"Yes. Plenty of births, deaths and scandals."

"Scandals. What kind of scandals?" I asked, my curiosity now aroused.

"Rumour has it," Mrs Tolson said, "that there was something of a scandal here years ago. Very handsome young groom and the mistress of the house"

"How long ago?" I enquired.

"I'm not sure, not sure at all. Maybe I'm thinking of something else or someone else. Just not sure," was her embarrassed reply, realising she may have committed a faux pas.

Together we carried the huge oil painting downstairs and Mrs Tolson gave it to great aunt Eliza Jane.

"Do you know who they are?" Mrs Tolson asked.

"I do indeed," replied my aunt. "It is my sister Letticia

Ann with her children Vera and Louisa when they were very young. This is your grandmother Bettina. Painted not long after Louisa, your mother, had her first birthday. That's her, the baby, and Vera is sitting on the pony."

I found myself looking into the eyes of an incredibly beautiful young woman with golden hair in a style known as 'The Gibson Girl Hairstyle'. Her lace blouse was of Edwardian design with a high collar. From her ears hung large ruby and diamond ear-rings. Her smile was one of utter contentment.

The children were laughing, rosy cheeked girls, one sitting on a Shetland pony; the other, little more than a baby sat on her mother's knee.

To the left of the painting, near the edge, stood a handsome young groom. He held the bridle of the pony but his eyes looked at Letticia Ann.

"I'll take it and have it cleaned," said aunt Eliza Jane. "It will look well in the hall at High Stones. My sister and her girls will be there for all to see. Thank you Freda I'm so glad you found it."

My aunt made no mention of the groom.

Driving back to High Stones I told my great aunt how interesting I had found the visit to my grandmother's house and could I ask her a favour.

The favour was to visit my grandfather's house in Northumberland and my request made her unquestionably uneasy.

"Are you sure about this?" she said, apprehensively stroking her five strand pearl necklace.

"Not if you really don't want to," I said, "but we wouldn't be going in, I just want to have a look and get a feel for the place."

The following day Adam drove us to Hexham. Aunt looked magnificent wearing her outfit which most matched that of Queen Mary, whom she greatly admired, adorned with an additional four strands of pearls, making nine in all. This I felt was a way of building her confidence as I was rapidly becoming aware that she did not wish to go. She kept telling me that she couldn't really remember where the house was as she had only been there once before. All most unusual for such an outgoing and usually self-assured woman.

We located a tea shop in the market square and I settled her down with scones and tea. The waitress was local so I asked her, "Do you happen to know where Ford House is, I understand it is a house on its own somewhere near here."

"Yes I do," she replied. "It's empty and up for sale, are you thinking of buying it ?"

"No," I said. "We used to know someone who lived there and I'm just curious to see it."

"That's a good thing," she said advisedly, "you wouldn't want to live there, it's haunted."

With my curiosity now fully stimulated I asked her for directions.

Adam negotiated the narrow country roads well and eventually, having driven through a shallow ford, we found ourselves in the right location. A 'For Sale' sign indicated the entrance.

Ford House was not only more than ten miles from Hexham but was well hidden away down a long, pitted, laurel lined drive which ended in the gloomy clearing of a wood. A huge, uninviting, pretentious, sombre looking grey stone house sat in the clearing and I immediately knew why my grandmother had not enjoyed living in this isolated place.

"You've seen it now, shall we go home?" Eliza said.

"You stay in the car and I'll have a closer look," I said, getting out of the car.

Walking towards the house I had the feeling of being watched. The waitress had told us that the property was empty so I became uneasy.

Looking through the ground floor windows, opaque with grime, I could see that the large rooms were uninhabited.

A tall, white haired, grey eyed man came along the front path of the house.

"How may I help you?" he said softly.

Unsure what to say I just explained that my grandparents had lived there several years ago and I was in the area and just wanted a look at the house and hoped he didn't mind.

"I don't mind at all my dear, please stay as long as you wish," he said, then went back along the path and disappeared around the corner of the house.

Turning back towards the limousine I noticed that Adam had moved the car ready to leave. I couldn't see aunt Eliza Jane because she was lying on the floor of the car and the moment I was back inside she quickly instructed Adam to drive away.

Once we were on the road to Newcastle I helped her lift herself back onto the seat. She looked slightly dishevelled and as white as a sheet.

"I know that man," she whispered. "It was Tobias Pym, your grandfather ... and he's been dead for thirty years."

"I'm very sorry aunt Eliza Jane," I said. "I hope you are not too upset."

"Nothing a stiff brandy won't put right," she said.

I had the distinct feeling that the death of my grandfather, Tobias Pym, and the mystery surrounding it, was a topic I would need to explore further. Perhaps not immediately though as great aunt Eliza Jane was clearly perturbed, which gave me the impression that when, initially, she had told me about him she had been somewhat economical with the truth.

On the last day of my visit Aunt Eliza Jane announced that she would be holding a small bon voyage soiree for me that evening. As we had been out and about every day there had been no time for cooking so the catering would be by a local restaurant who would also set out the food and clear away.

All the staff from the funeral business arrived and I was pleased to see they were not wearing black outfits. Along with some friends and neighbours the party was of about 25 guests. Gladys and Winnie both looked lovely, wearing similar full skirted red dresses; their husbands Cedric and Cyril were dressed identically as usual.

A butler, hired for the occasion, served champagne in the drawing room then the boom of the dinner gong signalled us into the dining room, from where tantalising aromas had been emitting for some time.

The Yemeni buffet was a delight to the eye and a complete surprise to me as I had only ever tasted British food. The table was a plethora of amazing spicy dishes all with names I could not pronounce. There was a lamb dish, a chicken platter, fish served complete with heads and tails. Mounds of fluffy rice, salads and flat breads; to be followed by delicious desserts of a honey cake with pistachios and small birds nest-like cakes each of which contained a date.

Aunt Eliza Jane introduced me to Aaron and Jamila who

ran the restaurant and Aaron's father, Mohammed, who was the owner.

I complimented them on the wonderful food and their response was one of gracious self-effacing modesty.

Aunt Eliza Jane later told me that Mohammed had been a seaman and settled in South Shields as a young man. His wife then joined him and that is where they raised their family.

Following the buffet, the entertainment was music and dancing in the hall which led to the swimming pool. Winnie and Gladys with their twin husbands were first to take to the dance floor to lead the party in a sedate waltz. They executed the dance with perfection, even changing partners from time to time with grace and ease, which delighted the party guests but confused me even more as I could not tell the twins apart. A gentleman asked me to dance and I was rather tense but just kept counting 123, 123 as we circled the floor.

Later Adam asked me to dance the foxtrot with him and I said, "I'd love to but I don't know it."

"Just follow me, I'll lead you," was his reply.

He took me in his arms and I followed him into a most wonderful experience of ballroom dancing. His hold was so secure and I did just as he had advised; he took the lead in the foxtrot, which I hoped would never end.

Sitting by the swimming pool, enjoying a refreshing lemonade following the foxtrot I asked him about his dancing skill.

"Oh I accompany ladies who don't have partners, at the tea dances in some of the big hotels, there is still a shortage of men around you know," he answered.

"So you are paid to dance with them?" I asked.

"Yes, the hotel pay me and I also play tennis with the ladies in the summer, also for money," he said.

"But I thought you were a driver at Gibbs Funeral Care!"
I exclaimed.

Adam laughed and said, "I am, but you see I need all the
money I can earn as I'm a student."

Tango music began to play and Winnie, Gladys with their
twin husbands took to the floor. Their tango dancing was
exquisitely passionate, making it difficult to believe they were
such quiet, sedate people in their day to day life as funeral
directors.

"Would you like to try?" Adam invited.

I surprised myself by accepting his invitation and the next
I knew we were swaying and kicking, tango style, to the music.

The whole evening had been fabulous; topped off by being held firmly by Adam for the last waltz which was wonderful and ended all too soon.

After all the guests had left aunt Eliza Jane questioned,
"So what do you think of our Adam then Bettina?"

I could feel myself blushing as I replied, in what I hoped
was a casual voice, "He seems nice and he's an extremely
good dancer."

"Oh he certainly is pet, and you could do a lot worse,"
she said.

"Oh, we only danced," I responded.

"I know my darling, but did he ask for your address?" she
said.

I then had to admit that he had and that I had given it to
him; but did not add that I was very much hoping to see him
again. Were I to be asked what was the highlight of my holiday I had no doubt that swimming in the heated pool would

be joint top of the list. Floating on my back looking up at the clouds through the glass atrium was totally relaxing; a treat I allowed myself each day following swimming several lengths.

Being held close by Adam was the other contender for top and I did wonder if he would contact me.

4

Providence House

On **returning to** Iona House there was a letter waiting for me. It was from my Aunt Agatha, who was my late father's sister.

Providence House,
Little Laxlet.

July 3rd, 1933.

Dear Bettina,

Sorry to bother you as I know you are kept busy with looking after John and Alfie and also working for Stan in the office. Mother is getting worse with her depression and memory loss and I'm having a bit of a struggle managing. Father helps where he can but he is nearly 90 now.
Please could you come for a visit to help me decide what is to be done.
The spare bedroom is made up if you want to stay the night.

Love,

Agatha.

I immediately answered Agatha's letter and said I would be with her the following Saturday and I would be bringing John and Alfie with me.

The boys enjoyed the train journey which they viewed as

something of an adventure. From Burside we took the bus to Little Laxlet.

As we walked through the village to Providence House so fierce was the mid-day summer heat that I noticed the tarmac road was starting to melt and bubble up. This reminded me of playing at bursting the tar bubbles as a child and mam chiding me and rubbing my tar smeared skin with butter paper to remove the mess. I made the decision not to tell my brothers of my tar bubble bursting escapades in case they had a similar idea.

Providence House was the residence my Grandparents moved to when they gave up their farm following the death of their two oldest sons in the Great War and then the death, from Spanish Flu, of my own father Alfred, their youngest son. The horses from the farm were also taken and lost in that war, so together they made the decision not to continue farming without their sons.

Approaching the house from across the village green, surrounded by pretty cottages, I was reminded what an incredibly beautiful stone property it was, more so it seemed to me, as it sat at the foot of a grassy bank, looking comfortably cool in the hot sun. A pretty cottage garden to the front, with the honeysuckle in full bloom, ascending the walls and embracing the windows. For a moment I was completely beguiled; breathing in the honeysuckle and rose infused air, I felt that time was standing still.

However this was to be a short lived pleasure as, on entering Providence House, my senses were accosted by an overpowering smell of dirt and decay, which was totally unexpected. It became obvious that this was one of the reasons Agatha had requested my visit.

Her smile and hugs welcomed us into the hall whilst simultaneously she was apologising for the shockingly filthy state of the house. As a woman of fastidiously clean disposition Agatha must have found living in such conditions almost unbearable.

I kept the boys close as we were led into the kitchen via a filthy door curtain which I did not wish them to touch. As we entered I noticed that every surface was covered with the detritus of life. The table in the centre of the room was piled, to ceiling height, with old newspapers. Agatha explained that grandfather used the newspaper pile as storage for various items which were important to him and which he may require at any moment. Bewildered we looked at this strange storage solution and could clearly see items such as his spectacles, a comb, his razor and shaving brush, a torch, a ruler, screwdriver, a saw and many other items all pushed between the layers of newspaper with just sufficient visible to identify the object.

I could see the convenience of such a system but the table could not be used as a table and there was the hazard of the whole pile falling onto someone and causing injury.

An enormous ball of flies languorously circulated above our heads which fascinated John and Alfie but which I found disgustingly disconcerting.

A small scullery, adjacent to the kitchen, was where Agatha prepared and cooked food. This room was clean and kept locked to prevent grandfather filling it with his junk.

"Where is grandmother?" I asked, hoping to move out of the kitchen.

"She has taken to her bed," Agatha replied, "Which is just as well; since dad became a hoarder it is too dangerous for her to leave her bedroom. He even brings things home that other people have thrown away."

Agatha made a cup of tea which we carried into the overgrown, but still beautiful, walled back garden. I encouraged the boys to explore and they quickly found trees to climb and outbuildings to investigate.

It was clear that coping with the old folk had become almost overwhelming for Agatha, now in her thirties and disabled herself. She had been born with a dislocated hip necessitating her to wear a heavy built up boot and she now suffered from back problems. Her pretty face, looked lined and furrowed, and her once dark brown hair was becoming prematurely grey.

"Where is grandfather?" I asked.

"Over at the Shoulder of Mutton,"(the village pub) was Agatha's reply. "Don't worry he only has a shandy which he doesn't consider to be alcohol. He enjoys a chat with the lads and usually brings some old rubbish home."

My grandparents were chapel folk and had always been teetotal so for grandfather to be visiting a pub came as quite a surprise.

Going back into the house the extent of the hoarding became even more apparent. Every room was stacked, ceiling high in places, with items of all descriptions and climbing the stairs was a dangerous task

The discernible smell of faeces met us as we entered grandmothers bedroom. Agatha explained that her mother was now incontinent.

I hardly recognised the tiny white haired old lady plucking at her bed sheets as my grandmother, so frail and shrunken she had become.

I said, "Hello granny, it's Bettina, I've come to visit you."

There was no response, she just stared through me and continued plucking at her bedding.

Agatha and I cleaned and washed granny then dressed her in fresh nightwear. She protested throughout, vehemently accusing us of torturing her, in a loud reproachful voice.

"Will she sit in the chair for a while?" I asked Agatha.

"She might," was Agatha's reply, "But only if I give her a glass of sherry and a cigarette."

"I had no idea she smoked or drank," I said, feeling quite shocked.

"It's the only way to get her to co-operate, bribery I suppose, but she thinks the sherry is medicine," Agatha replied.

I had no wish to criticize Agatha on the care she was giving in such difficult circumstances so granny was helped into the chair, given her glass of sherry, she then puffed away happily on a cigarette.

Whilst we changed the bed I asked Agatha how she coped with the laundry.

"Our neighbour, Mrs Davis, comes by each day to collect it and she kindly washes all the bedding and towels. I do the rest by hand,

I'm not sure how much longer I can continue on my own with father hoarding and mother so demented, that is why I asked you to come to see us. What can be done?" This was Agatha's despondent explanation followed by her penetrative question regarding a solution.

Before I could reply John and Alfie came rushing into the bedroom.

"Look, look we found a frog," they shouted as the frog leapt out of John's hands and onto the hearthrug.

Grandmother began to laugh and then gently chastised the boys saying, "How many times have I told you Joseph not to bring frogs into the house. Now catch the poor thing and put it back into the pond."

My grandmother thought John was her own son Joseph who had died in 1917 fighting at the battle of Passchendale in the Great War. This I found worryingly sad, but to see the way her face lit up when she saw the boys had, obviously, given her a moment of joy.

My mind was racing, trying to formulate an acceptable plan which would help, without causing offence, to liberate Agatha and ameliorate the situation.

When grandfather came home from the pub Agatha and I discussed the problems with him and he agreed that I should contact Stan and arrange for him to help with the arduous task of clearing some of the hoard.

I then, tentatively, raised the possibility of employing a nurse to help to care for granny but his response to this was one of total refusal and opposition to any idea of extra help.

The walk in the summer sunshine to the telephone box on the village green was a pleasure after breathing the cloyingly putrid air inside Providence House.

Passing Groat Cottage John pointed and said, "Didn't we used to live there, in that cottage?"

"Yes," I replied, "But we had to move to Iona House after mam died."

"Do you think my bike is still in the back yard?" John asked. "Can we go and look when you've phoned Stan?"

I telephoned Stan who said he would come to Little Laxlet the following day.

The boys and I then walked across the village green,

passed the pretty cottages and houses, all with stone walled enclosed gardens which were in full bloom.

My knock on the door of Groat Cottage received no response so we called to see Hilda, now a widow, who lived next door and whom we had known all our lives. She was delighted to see us and immediately commented on how much both boys had grown.

As far as she knew the Flitches still had the tenancy next door.

Over a cup of tea Hilda said, "It's strange, no one seems to be living in Groat Cottage but I do hear people coming and going during the night."

The cottages were attached with a party wall.

I didn't develop the conversation in front of the boys but made the decision to further investigate at a later date.

The back yard at my old home was empty with the exception of the tin bath still hanging on its hook on the wall. We looked in the coal-house but, disappointingly for John, his bike was not there.

Bedtime at Providence House was great fun for John and Alfie who made the decision to sleep in camp beds in the hayloft above the old stable. The stable was now an immaculate studio with a four poster bed, chaise long and full length mirror.

Agatha and I sat in the overgrown garden when the boys had gone to bed and she told me that she had converted the old stable into a studio for herself. It was where she found peace and tranquillity, making her pillow lace away from the main house. Her friend, Frank, sometimes visited and as the house was too messy for guests they would meet and spend time in the comfort of the studio.

My interest was aroused and I asked Agatha more about Frank.

Without a shred of self-consciousness she told me, "Frank is a pharmacist and we are lovers."

"Real lovers," was my eye popping response. "You mean you have *sex*?"

Then I felt stupid because that is what lovers do.

"Oh yes," she said, with a dreamy, coy smile, "we have monumentally fantastic sex most Wednesday afternoons and Sundays when the chemist shop is closed."

"Really," I commented. Now fully realising the purpose of the four poster bed.

"Yes really," she continued. "Making love to someone you love and knowing they feel the same way about you is truly amazing."

"It sounds wonderful," I said.

"With the weather being so warm this summer," Agatha continued, "we have occasionally been known to strip naked and make love in the garden by the light of the moon."

"Naked, *totally* naked?" I asked.

"Yes naked, totally naked. Afterwards we lie there, on our blanket, replete from our passion for each other, enjoying the night sky. Frank is interested in astronomy and I'm learning a lot about it now."

Surprisingly, I did not feel embarrassed at all, only astounded that my Aunt Agatha, now in her early thirties, could speak so openly about being in a sexual relationship.

"Are you planning on a wedding in the future?" was my next question. Hoping that the answer would not contain complications such as that Frank was already married.

"We are just happy as we are," was her reply. "Anyway

you'll meet Frank tomorrow, it's Sunday.

The croaking frogs and occasional hoot of a lone owl lulled me to sleep but my mind was still full of the thoughts of aunt Agatha having a lover and, there I was, spending the night in Agatha's bed, in her studio, which was their love nest.

5

Garden Spruce Up

The following morning a soft knocking at the door of the stable studio woke me; Agatha entered with tea, scrambled eggs on toast and strawberries. John and Alfie climbed down the ladder from the hay loft and we enjoyed breakfast, all of us, in the big four poster bed with Agatha.

"It is so good to have you here," Agatha said. "I don't suppose you have come up with a long term solution which father would agree to?"

"Not yet, but you never know, today we might just think of something," I replied, hoping any lack of conviction would not be evident in my voice.

Stan arrived at around 10am in his ex Huntly and Palmer delivery van and together we assessed the hoarding situation in the house. I explained that my grandfather had agreed to clearing the hoard to make the house safe but not to any nursing help with grandmother.

Always practical; Stan's accurate appraisal had quickly concluded that more than one clearing session would be required to make the house safe.

We looked at the hoard and made the decision that to clear the kitchen would be a good place to start.

Reversing the van into the driveway at the side of the property was of great interest to grandfather who insisted, unnecessarily, on guiding Stan in and coming perilously close to the moving wheels.

"That's a fine van thas got there lad," he commented.

"Thanks Mr Dawson," Stan replied, opening the big back doors of the van.

"Carry a lot of stuff it would," grandfather commented, leaning on his stick and looking inside the van.

"It does," said Stan. "I've come to move some stuff from the house for you, to make it easier to move around. Shall we go in and you can show me what you want me to take away?"

Thankfully grandfather had agreed to me taking down the filthy door curtain before we entered the kitchen to make the decision about removing things.

However, every item either Stan or I suggested for removal he had a reason why it should stay.

Clinging to us like a limpet he ordered, "Nothing to be removed from the kitchen."

We all moved into the hall.

"Nothing to be removed from the hall," he said again. His limpet mode persisting.

It was the same in the dining room, living room and the spare bedrooms.

Following an explanation from me regarding safety he agreed to us removing some items from the stairs.

This all took over an hour and no progress was being made. Everything to him had a value and a memory, even his piles of old newspapers. He just kept saying no to anything other than those few items from the stairs. Losing his three sons, his horses and grandmother now not the person he once knew, perhaps holding on to old junk made him feel secure.

"As I said afore Stan, that's a grand van thas got there,

shame to tak it away empty. Mother loves this garden, could you maybe tidy it up for her. I'd really appreciate that lad, the house'll do fine for now but t' garden needs a tidy and I'm past it, the gardening," grandfather said.

"The garden it is then," Stan replied, realising he was beaten with regard to the hoard.

The sound of a bicycle bell attracted our attention and a pretty young woman with a long, thick blond plait, aged I would guess, in her late twenties, wheeled her cycle passed the van and parked it outside the kitchen door. In the basket attached to the handlebars was a large lidded dish containing a hearty lunch of lamb hot pot enough to feed us all, along with several loaves of crusty bread which she carried in her rucksack.

"Bettina, I'd like to introduce you to Frank," Agatha said, shepherding the blond haired young woman towards me.

"I'm really Francine," Frank commented, "but everyone calls me Frank.

Frank was dressed in trousers and a short sleeved pink blouse in readiness she told me, "to help with the clearing up." However, I could see that she had lovely high cheek bones, a full sensitive mouth and a tiny waist, so throughout lunch my mind wandered to imagining sex between her and Agatha.

Absolutely unaware of same sex relationships I wondered if the chaise long and full length mirror were part of their love making. They acted as good friends and I would not have suspected that they were lovers had Agatha not told me.

Stan took charge of the garden 'tidy up' giving us all a job to do. We found some old tools in the apple store and these, combined with the ones he had brought, kept us all busy.

Mrs Davis called to collect the laundry and stopped to have a chat. During our conversation I tentatively enquired whether she might be willing to work some hours each day to help with grandmother.

"Of course I would," was her reply, "and my boys are always on hand if needed."

She told me she was the widow of a police inspector and that she had five sons, all of whom wished to be police officers.

"My two oldest boys, Bryn, after his father and Emrys are already in the force," she said.

"How old are they?" I enquired.

"Bryn is 25 years, Emrys 22 years, Gwilym 19 years, Gareth 17 years and my baby Owen 15 years. They are wonderful sons but I still miss my Bryn even after 11years of being on my own."

"They sound fantastic," I said. "Perhaps we might meet them."

"Oh yes, I think Gwilym might pop over to give a hand this afternoon," she replied.

"That will be nice and I'll have a word with grandfather about some extra time you might have to help Agatha with grandmother."

Gwilym, Gareth and Owen all came over to Providence House to help and by 4pm the garden looked much clearer and the pond was now fully visible. The stone walls were warm from the heat of the sun and already tiny apples and pears were forming on the espaliered fruit trees. The van was full of garden rubbish but I did notice that grandfather had removed the items we had cleared from the stairs and they were now back in the house.

In the stable studio Agatha asked me to look at the lace she had made and now stored there.

"I keep it here away from the mess in the house, but I worry that in the winter the stable might be damp or the harvest mice will damage the lace," she explained to Frank and me, adding, "I have an ambition that one day my lace will be incorporated in beautiful silk underwear, but that's a bit of a dream at the moment."

Gorgeous mounds of hand made lace covered the bed and we all agreed that to allow it to be spoiled by damp or mice would be sacrilege.

"Would it help if I took the lace back to Iona House and stored it in my sewing room?" I asked.

Agatha obviously trusted me as she agreed that this would probably be the best solution under the circumstances.

"I've had a word with Mrs Davis and she is willing to help with grandmother," I explained. "and I shall sound grandfather out before we leave, but don't build your hopes up."

Frank said, "Thank you so much Bettina, Agatha really needs help and so far her father has refused. I hope you can influence him."

We found a couple of rugs and some old garden chairs and decided that a reward of sitting under the old apple tree to enjoy some lemonade would be a good idea. Hilda brought sandwiches across from her cottage and Mrs Davis brought her famous fruit cake for which, I was told, she had won prizes at the county show in the past.

Traditionally, in Little Laxlet, fruit cake would be eaten with Wensleydale cheese but in the Davis household Pembrokeshire cheddar was the cheese of choice. Mrs Davis's sister in law regularly sent a supply by train from Wales for her five nephews. The boys seemed happy to share and we all enjoyed the Welsh cheese with the prize winning cake that afternoon. Personally I preferred Wensleydale but felt it would be discourteous to comment.

I could see grandfather was in a mellow mood so took the opportunity to ask about Mrs Davis helping Agatha with grandmother.

"Ay lass, just what I was thinking me sen," was his response, "now don't you think that's a grand idea?"

Mrs Davis had gone upstairs into the house to see to grandmother and we heard a knocking on the landing window. When we turned, there was my grandmother, supported by Mrs Davis and Gwilym looking out at the garden granny loved so much, I glanced across at my grandfather and there were tears in his eyes.

As we were leaving I promised Agatha that when the boys were on their summer school holidays we would come back and then perhaps grandfather might allow us to clear away some of the rubbish in the house.

I hugged my dear old grandfather and said that I would visit again soon and his response was, "Tha needs a car Bettina, that would make it easier for you to come and see us. Stan please look into getting a little car for Bettina and I'm sure you could show her how to go on with t' driving. Don't tha worry about t' price, I'll pay, just don't go overboard. Remember I'm only a poor old farmer."

It was the longest speech I'd ever heard my grandfather make as he was renowned for being a man of few words and careful with money. So I wasn't entirely certain he meant what he said or that perhaps it might be the emotion of the day.

When John and Alfie were safely tucked into the old arm chairs, which were bolted to the floor in the back of the van, a frog croaked which made us laugh.

Surrounded by garden rubbish and with Agatha's big box of lace on my knee we all, including the frog, headed back to Ransington which was now home; but I knew my heart belonged to Little Laxlet.

6

The Dress

Dora, Ian's wife and sister-in-law to Angus and Vera had hinted some months before that Ian would be appointed, in the summer of 1933, by the Lord Chamberlain's Office, to be a Crown Court Judge. In celebration of this, she had decided to hold a family party in the grounds of their huge mansion, Hampton House out at Mallard Hall, an exclusive suburb of Ransington. Weather permitting, the evening party would be held in the garden and, although she would be having caterers to provide and serve the food; I'd been told by Vera that Dora had requested my help, but had not specified in her telephone message in what way.

A small orchestra with an operatic soloist was to be part of her arrangements, as was a magnificent cake which was to be the centre piece of the table; so far that is all I knew.

I prepared for Dora's visit, (or preliminary planning meeting as she called it) in my beautiful tower office/sewing room by opening all the windows. Dora seemed blissfully ignorant of how unpleasant her cigarette smoke was for others and would always smoke several of her black cigarettes irrespective of where, or with whom, she was.

Arriving on time and in her usual forthright manner she, predictably and immediately, 'lit up' a black Russian cigarette and placed it in a mother of pearl holder; our meeting commenced with her saying, "Bettina I will require you to be incredibly organised as I have so much to do, and this party for Ian must be perfect in every way."

"So what is it you have in mind for me to do?" was my question.

Focusing her penetrative blue eyes on me she commenced with, "Initially I would like you to make 50 monogrammed table napkins plus bunting, lots of bunting. Stan is spending a great deal of time making the garden look wonderful and I plan to have bunting and fairy lights in the trees. I will also ask you, nearer the time, to arrange the fresh flowers for the table decorations. You can make them here of course and Stan will bring them over to Hampton House in his van." She hardly drew breath.

Dora had come fully prepared for the meeting, making copious notes in a beautiful red Chinese silk covered notebook, using her gold nibbed Parker fountain pen. I could see she had long lists and my name was at the top of at least two of them. She began to pace about the room, supposedly discussing the party which, to my mind, became more fanciful with each sentence she uttered. A proposed ice sculpture was mentioned as was further entertainment of a magician and fireworks. As she wandered about my beautiful tower room, conveying her instructions, I followed, ensuring the ash tray was within her reach at all times.

I thought the meeting was over when suddenly she almost shouted, "There is also another event with which I may require your help."

My heart sank.

"I'm not sure if you are aware," she said, "that I am now a governor at The Alpine Lodge Orphanage. There is to be a charity fete in the grounds in August, which being a month away gives us oodles of time Bettina. Again I would just love it if you were in charge of the bunting and again, plenty of it. Also perhaps a raffle prize or two, to raise money for those poor, dear orphan boys and girls. Did I mention that I'm now on the board there and you know how much I adore children."

'Adore children' I thought, 'she never came anywhere near when John, Alfie and Claudette were so ill with whooping cough.'

For a moment I was robbed of speech, then I heard myself saying "I'll see what I can do", a rather lame comment I acknowledge, whilst thinking, 'this will put my new idea for a quilt on hold again' and trying not to allow my face to look sulky.

"Oh, I know I can rely on you Bettina, shall we meet again, say in one week, to discuss progress? Must fly now, I have an appointment with my ladies on the League of Health and Beauty committee and I just know they will be extremely enthusiastic to contribute."

I wondered if Dora irritated the Health and Beauty ladies as much as she did me. Then I gave myself a good talking to, along the lines of:- 'Ian is a really good, kind man and deserves a party to celebrate his success at being appointed a judge. Dora can't help the way she is, just look forward to what promises to be a lovely party'.

Having been mentioned in the New Years Honours list Angus now had the date for the investiture at Buckingham Palace and it was drawing closer; the dress code for gentlemen was top hat and tails and for ladies smart day wear. Vera was in a quandary on two counts, one being her attire for the big day and the other was her concern about leaving Rory, now 10 months old. He had been breast fed from birth and was now starting to enjoy some weaning food; but compared to other babies seemed to me to be extremely clingy. So much so that he screamed and cried when ever he could not see his mother or whoever was caring for him at the time.

The decision was made by Vera that Rory would be weaned from breast feeding onto bottle feeding as a necessary requirement of her accompanying Angus to his investiture.

A tin of Dr Leiburg's formula was purchased and thankfully he seemed to enjoy the new milk and drinking from a bottle. Gradually bottle replaced breast feeding and when the time came for Vera and Angus to travel to London he was fully bottle fed; and happy to accept Vera, Bonny or myself feeding him.

Vera's outfit for the 'big day' proved to be somewhat more of a problem.

Following Dora's suggestion, I accompanied Vera to Fiskers; a dress shop in Ransington selling designer garments for exclusive clients attending exclusive events. (Dora's words) Fiskers gave a guarantee that there would only ever be one garment made of each design.

Vera tried on several smart day dresses with matching hats but none seemed perfect and she wanted to look especially elegant for such an important occasion.

My dressmakers eye could see that the dresses were indeed well made but the prices were extortionate. No doubt, I thought, to cover the wages of the supercilious staff, the gold encrusted sofas and the glass of cheap, faux champagne.

"I just don't seem to be in the mood to shop for clothes," Vera sighed in an exhausted tone, "but I will have to buy something new for such a special day."

We had wandered into the department store and the tea room beckoned.

Over a cuppa our conversation returned to 'the dress' and Vera took me completely by surprise by saying, "Could you possibly make it for me Bettina?"

"That would be quite a responsibility," was my answer.

"You are more than up to it, come on let's go and look at patterns and fabric." She had visibly cheered up.

The pale blue crepe de chine fabric rippled across the dining room table, then settled, in readiness to receive the pattern for pinning.

My afternoons now became a focus of making a dress befitting Lady Vera McLeod accompanying her husband to meet the King at Buckingham Palace.

'No pressure there then!' I thought.

Mrs Scribbins, our washerwoman, was very interested in how the dressmaking project was progressing and keen to be of help.

"I 'av every confidence in your dressmaking Miss Bettina," she commented as together, on washday, we hung out the wet laundry in the garden to dry.

"Av you got a tailors dummy? Ever so elpful, I'm told if you're dressmaking."

"I agree Mrs Scribbins," I replied, "and no I don't have one."

"Mrs Arrison, where I cleans on a Friday, as one and if I asks er she might just lend hit to you. Shall I ask er for you?"

Stan collected the tailors dummy and carried it up the winding staircase into the tower room, which continued to be my favourite room in the house. The tailors dummy would now be a permanent feature as Mrs Harrison no longer made clothes.

Each morning I would need to focus on the office work for Stan's business then the afternoons would be taken up with sewing Vera's dress, until it was time to collect the boys from school.

The dress was a joy to make and the dressmakers dummy an enormous help. The crepe fabric, some cut on the bias, fell smoothly into folds in the mid-calf length lined skirt. The close fitting bodice had a large satin collar, with a three button detail, in a slightly deeper shade of blue which toned with the crepe perfectly. Three quarter length sleeves and a 2 inch wide belt with a silver buckle completed the ensemble.

Vera looked wonderful in her blue dress, matching tiny hat with a small curled feather which perched, slightly tilted,as was the fashion that year, on the side of her brown hair which she wore in a soft roll. Her navy shoes, handbag and gloves completed the outfit.

Percy drove Angus and Vera to the railway station in the Bentley, where they caught the train to London. They travelled first class with steward service and enjoyed an amazingly good lunch in the pull-man coach as they journeyed south.

Their accommodation in London was two nights at the Ritz hotel.

Having read about the hotel in a magazine, this to me, was the epitome of grandiose luxury.

Vera told us, on her return, that Buckingham Palace was an interesting building but that Angus had not met the King who was unwell. Edward, Prince of Wales stood in for King George V that day and it was the Prince who had knighted Uncle Angus.

Staying at the Ritz hotel had been wonderful, as were the cocktails followed by dinner and dancing until late.

"It was rather like a second honeymoon." was the way Vera wistfully described the trip.

During their absence Bonny and I looked after the children and I did notice that, although Rory was accepting of either of us as a substitute for his mother, he became extremely upset if neither of us was within his visual field.

Whenever the doorbell rang or a tradesman knocked on the kitchen door Claudette would run into the hall or kitchen, curious to see who was there. Rory appeared not to notice which made me feel concerned as to whether he had some hearing loss.

One day he was playing quietly and absorbed with his toys I dropped a tin pot behind him hoping he would respond by turning to the sound – he did not!

I expressed my concerns to Bonny and, whilst Claudette was 'helping' Mrs Handyside, we played a game with him. Bonny sat in front of Rory and distracted him with his favourite toys and I made noises to each side of him in such a way that he could respond and turn to the sound – he did not respond.

My suspicions were confirmed – Rory did have hearing loss and I would need to tell his parents on their return.

7

Rosa-Lee

A stifling heat wave swept the country in August 1933, causing the children to become fractious with each other. Claudette, now approaching her second birthday was an assertive child and inclined to 'melt down' when thwarted. Her favourite word being no!

Rory's hearing loss was a huge concern for Angus and Vera who sought advice and help from a specialist audiologist and an ear, nose and throat consultant.

Stan, now busier than ever with his gardening business, also helped his dad with the Iona House gardens and worked two days each week for Dora and Ian. He had taken on a lad to assist him and his mother, Mrs Handyside, was delighted with the success of her son 'the entrepreneur', as she called him. I had begun to find the office work tryingly onerous as each morning and, now some afternoons, I laboured in the heat with Stan's schedules, quotes and invoices.

"How would you like to learn to type?" Vera asked. "Think how much quicker it would be dealing with the paper work."

I knew a typewriter would be a brilliant addition to the office as I was finding it tediously slow, having to hand-write everything.

A spare typewriter was brought from the Landsdown Short offices and Miss Iris Mathias, Head of the typing pool would be calling every Friday afternoon to teach me how to use it.

The following Friday at 2pm precisely I opened the door to a plump pretty lady, aged about 40 years. who was visibly sweating in the extreme heat of the afternoon. The climb up into the tower room office was clearly a trial for Iris; her breathlessness and excessive perspiration bore testament to this.

On arrival in the office I offered Iris a drink of cold water; then, sitting in the shade by an open window she, thankfully, made a fairly quick recovery.

She said, "I've had no time for lunch, do you mind if I eat whilst I teach? As it's Friday I'm meeting my boyfriend in the park and we are going for a trip on the boating lake."

I, of course, told her that I did not mind.

"Just a snack, I feel quite faint if I go too long without food," she said, opening her bag which contained a huge pork pie which she ate with relish, followed by an Eccles cake, 4 ginger biscuits and a large piece of cheese..

I refilled her glass with water and in an effort to be polite, then enquired, "What's your boyfriend's name?"

"Well he's really my fiancé, we've been engaged for 15years near enough, although it's not official, been on and off over the years and his name is Mr Chapman -Mr Jeremiah Chapman," she sighed. "Feels the cold he does, I expect he'll be wearing his tweed suit, waistcoat and cap today and in this heat, it must be in the 80s."

To show interest I enquired as to when the wedding would be.

"Next year – for definite next year," she replied, "but heaven only knows how we'll get on in bed, me so hot and him always freezing cold."

"Oh! I'm sure you'll be fine," I responded, thinking they could make a perfect couple, especially if he likes pork pies.

She must have read my thoughts as her next statement was, "Mr Chapman is a most fussy eater, I blame his mother for that, thin as a stick he is, not a picking on him."

A mental picture of Mr Chapman was now forming in my mind.

"We did have a weekend away in Scarborough last year but his bitch of a mother insisted on coming with us, and what's more she sat in the front of the car next to Mr Chapman leaving me to sit in the back, I felt quite affronted."

"How did the weekend work out?" I enquired, not feeling confident that it would have been a huge success.

"Well *SHE* put a real dampener on things, I can tell you. Insisted on sharing a bed with me, I was furious, furious. I'd bought all new sexy undies, tap pants in silky rayon and a negligee from Woolworths which I just knew would thrill Mr Chapman," Iris said.

"That must have been disappointing for you both," was all I could think to say in response.

"Certainly was, especially as he was well up for it and so was I. If his mother thinks she is coming on honeymoon with us she can just think again," said Iris.

"Perhaps you could elope to Gretna Green," I suggested.

"Good idea, either that or I might just have to lock her in the cellar for a week," she joked, dabbing 'Evening in Paris' perfume behind her ears. The aroma of which, she assured me, would drive Mr Chapman into a wild sensuous passion and his mother would be out at the pictures that evening.

"With a bit of luck we'll be in ecstasy-land in her double bed before she's even seen the Pathe news!"

"*Her* double bed?" I enquired, wondering if I'd heard correctly.

"Oh, yes. Mr Chapman only has a single with a flat wooden head board. Useless for handcuffs, he loves the handcuffs Mr Chapman does. Her bed has brass rods, top and bottom – perfect! Mind you he keeps his cap and socks on at all times!"

Miss Mathias, (as she preferred to be addressed, first names being too familiar for her) then explained to me the mysteries of the qwerty keyboard, carbon paper and how to change a typewriter ribbon without covering oneself and everything else with ink.

On leaving she assured me that I would soon become confident and proficient in the use of the typewriter giving me the distinct impression that she had no wish to climb the steep staircase again.

Returning to my office there was the distinct whiff of pork pie in the air combined with 'Evening in Paris' perfume, a smell which I will always associate with my one and only typing lesson.

Once again my patchwork and quilting was put on hold due to bunting making for Dora's fund raising event for the orphanage. I also made cushion covers, and bought the pads to fill them, for raffle prizes. Eventually the bunting and cushions were made and awaiting collection by Dora.

The day before the fete I was awoken at 6:30am by a telephone call, it was Dora, "Bettina, please be an angel and pop to the orphanage this morning with the bunting and prizes as I'm 'up to my eyes' as you might imagine. My ladies from the League of Health and Beauty will be over there and will hang the bunting on my behalf. Mrs Barnes is in charge of the raffle so just hand the raffle prizes to her to deal with."

I took John and Alfie with me to Alpine Lodge Orphanage and explained to them, as I walked and they scootered, that the children they would probably meet lived together because they had no family to take care of them.

Instantaneously I did not like the place at all, so institutionalised, smelling of disinfectant and boiled cabbage. The pale faced girls, all dressed the same, dull eyed and expressionless, some with snotty noses, huddled around the House Mother. The boys, again all dressed the same, were playing football on the field and invited John and Alfie to join in.

I found Dora's League of Health and Beauty ladies setting up stalls in readiness for the fete the following day and I asked them if they knew where Dora was, but they were unsure.

Then one lady said, "At the hairdressers, I think."

I left with John and Alfie as soon as I could; the place sent shivers down my spine and was not somewhere I wished to spend a moment longer than I needed to.

On our walk back to Iona House I discussed the orphanage with the boys and they seemed not to have gained the same impression as me, having been engaged in the football game and knowing some of the boys as they all went to the same school.

A few days later Mrs Handyside said, "I hear Dora's orphanage fete was a big success, raised quite a bit of money to take the children on trips to the seaside, so I'm told."

"That's good news," was my response, thinking that, 'there but for the goodness of Vera and Angus, John and Alfie could be living at Alpine Lodge Orphanage.'

Although, technically, they were not actually orphans as their father, Herbert Flitch was still alive, but he had abandoned them!

A few days following the fete the Gazette ran an article about the success of the event with a picture of Dora with the Mayor and other Civic dignitaries.

As for Dora, she didn't even have the good manners to thank me for the bunting and cushions, which came as no surprise to me at all!

During the week before the party at Hampton House it had been arranged for Dora to meet with Mr Handyside our gardener and myself to discuss selecting flowers for her table decorations. Whilst waiting for her I answered a knock on the kitchen door to find a young gypsy woman standing on the step selling her wares.

"Fine bilberries, willow pegs and lucky white heather," she said. "Always good to buy from Rosa-lee, everyth'n fresh picked from the moor only this morn'n."

I purchased bilberries and clothes pegs and then I saw her eyeing the remaining money in my purse.

"Cross me palm with silver for your fortune to be told," she said.

I did not believe in fortune tellers and had never had my fortune told but found myself placing a silver three penny piece in the palm of her hand.

She looked at me for what seemed like an eternity then spoke very quietly.

"In 12 moons I see a phoenix bird."

"What does that mean?" I enquired.

"Rosa-lee only tells what she sees. In 12 moons I see a phoenix bird."

To me this made no sense and not very good value for my silver three penny piece so I asked her to tell me anything else she might see.

"The babby is swaddled and crying, poor might," she said.

Bonny had taken Claudette and Rory to the park and John and Alfie were out playing football so I knew there were no children in the house.

She repeated, "The babby is swaddled and crying."

I was about to ask her more but Dora arrived and immediately expressed shock and horror to find me talking to a gypsy.

"What on earth has possessed you to engage with a dirty gypsy woman?" she shrieked at me.

Addressing the gypsy she shouted, "GET AWAY FROM HERE AND DON'T EVER COME BACK. THIEVES AND VAGABONDS, THAT'S WHAT YOU ARE. LEAVE AT ONCE!"

A dignified Rosa-lee picked up her basket and, as she did, spoke quietly in a strange tongue, it sounded like a chant; all the time looking straight at Dora.

A bee settled on a sprig of white heather which the gypsy handed to me with the bee still in situ.

"All-us listen to the bees miss, and I thank ee," she said, then smiled at me as she left.

8

A Diamond Necklace

The following Saturday was the day of the party at Hampton House in celebration of Ian becoming a Judge.

I went downstairs into the kitchen to find the table covered with flowers and foliage from the gardens of Iona House.

Dora had again visited the previous day and further instructed Mr Handyside as to which blooms she wanted for the table decorations, not wishing to pick any from her own garden.

Mrs Handyside looked in and said, "I've just called in to say our Stanley will be picking up the table decorations and bunting at about noon. That Dora has him running around after her like I don't know what – thinks she owns him, she does."

"I haven't seen much of Stan lately," I said.

"No wonder, he's been at her beck and call up at Hampton House. Takes him away from his work, I don't like it, I really don't like it."

"Well I expect she wants her garden looking lovely for the party this evening and there's nothing Stan doesn't know about gardening," I commented, thinking that would cheer her up.

Mrs Handyside sniffed, "Well I hope it's just the garden

and not designs on him."

"Designs on Stan?" I was shocked at the thought of it and said, as much to reassure myself as her, "but Dora and Ian are very happy together, you told me that yourself. Also I would have thought Stan was far too young for Dora."

"Time will tell, time will tell," said Mrs Handyside with foreboding in her voice.

At noon Stan called for the table decorations and bunting and I don't know if I imagined it but he seemed very chirpy, spinning me round and planting a big kiss on my lips.

"Hello stranger," I said. "What's put a spring in your step?"

"Lovely sunny day, party tonight. It should be good, we can have a dance on Dora's wooden dance floor in the garden. Plenty of free beer and a kiss and cuddle with my favourite girl – what more could a chap ask for?"

"But I'm not going to the party," I responded, assuming that I was his favourite girl. "I'll be looking after the children whilst Vera and Angus go."

"That's a shame," he said unconvincingly, loading the table decorations into his van. "Toodle oo then," he called.

'Toodle oo then', I thought. That doesn't sound sincere. His mother could be right, perhaps there is someone else who is now Stan's 'favourite girl!'

Vera looked exquisitely beautiful, wearing the blue crepe de chine dress I had made her for the investiture. She and Angus had had such a worrying time with Rory and his deafness that, although I did feel sad I was not going to the party, I hoped they would have a lovely evening.

Ian had given Dora the gift of a stunning Edwardian diamond necklace to celebrate the occasion. This piece of jewellery had the capacity to either be worn as a necklace or a tiara and was incredibly valuable. During the days before the party Dora took great delight in trying it on first as a necklace then a tiara and had the enormous dilemma of not being able to make up her mind which way to wear it for the occasion. This problem constantly consumed her thoughts and during her visit to the hairdressers she tried it on as a tiara with her blond Marcel wave hairstyle arranged to suit.

Eventually, and moments before the arrival of the first guest, she made the decision to wear it as a necklace. After all, she thought, there would be many future occasions where more formal attire would be required and for which the tiara would be perfect.

The garden at Hampton House looked wonderful. Dora and Ian welcomed their, Master of Ceremonies announced, guests on arrival; two butlers served champagne whilst three waitresses served canapés. A six piece orchestra played light but dignified music as pre-arranged by Dora and the fairy lights twinkled in the trees.

The guests enjoyed a splendid dinner of salmon terrine, Aberdeen Angus beef with local vegetables followed by raspberry pavlova and cream. Wine flowed throughout the meal; during which the diners were entertained by a lady soprano singing light opera.

Ian made a short speech in which he thanked his wife for her support then the tempo of the music changed and those who wished to, took to the dance floor.

A magician, one 'Grand Magico' circulated around the tables impressing the guests with his magic tricks. He not only used cards, doves, silk handkerchiefs and rabbits, but could also remove a watch, wallet or other personal item without the owner even realising it had gone. Always found, often behind the ear or in the top pocket of a neighbouring diner.

As Ian took Dora into his arms and onto the dance floor, he considered he must be the luckiest man in the world to be married to a woman whom, he knew was not without faults, but he loved her as much in that moment as he had on the day they were married. (Vera had previously told me that his love for Dora was blind and always had been.)

As they danced she was in constant communication with her own importance and reflected on how successful the evening was. There could be no doubt that everyone would consider her an exemplary hostess, so successful, wearing her grey chiffon dress which draped so perfectly over her bust and toned thighs, complimenting her flawless skin and diamonds exquisitely.

A judge for a husband and living in such a fine house in a salubrious location, Dora felt she had reached the pinnacle within her social circle. Some degree of effort had been required, but all worth it.

All the guests had left by 1:30am.

At about 3am Ian left his bed to investigate a noise which had woken him. Picking up a heavy candlestick from the landing table he crept quietly down the stairs.

Noticing that the two, four feet high, Imperial Chinese floor vases had been moved from either side of the bottom of the staircase and were beside the front door along with the yellow and green Christopher Dresser jardinière and stand he immediately realised a burglary was in progress.

Crossing the hall, and just before losing consciousness from the blow to the back of his head, he was also aware that the glass doors to the hall cabinet were open and the silver had been removed.

Secure in the knowledge that Ian was unconscious the burglars silently and quickly went upstairs; one skilfully opening and emptying the safe which was behind an oil painting of Dora. The other looking for the diamond necklace, hoping to find it on the dressing table.

What stopped the burglar in his tracks was the sight of Dora lying on her back, naked apart from her diamond necklace, sound asleep on the bed. For a woman of her age, he estimated her to be late thirties, he considered her to be one of the most youthful and beautiful he had ever seen and began to feel a stirring in his loins causing a slight audible moan to escape from his lips.

A moment of weakness which soon passed; then skilfully and without any awareness from Dora, he removed the necklace from her throat. Should she wake and see him, he would, in one movement lasting only two seconds, break her neck as only a trained assassin can.

One final glimpse at her beauty, lying there in the heat of the night, wearing only the silver moonlight as it shone in through the open window, he gently kissed her forehead then departed as silently as he had arrived.

The two burglars quietly left the premises, driving away with the silver from the display case in the hall, the Imperial Chinese vases, Christopher Dresser jardinière and stand, the loot from the safe and the main prize of the diamond necklace ,in a catering van which had been hidden in the trees.

The blow had not killed Ian and he regained conciousness about an hour after the attack feeling kaleidoscopically dizzy and with a severe headache. His first thoughts were for Dora and his two boys. All were safe and had slept through the disturbance.

Fortunately he had previously had the foresight to photograph his valuable items and these photographs were later given to the police to help in their search.

9

The County Show

Following the party and the burglary, Ian made a good physical recovery but emotionally he had been traumatised by the event. He spent a good deal of time talking to Angus, which seemed to help him, but he kept worrying and saying he felt guilty as he had not protected his family. Extra security was installed at Hampton House and there was talk regarding a guard dog. The atmosphere at Iona House was rather solemn because of this, so I was delighted when a letter arrived for me from my friend Ada.

> *Rookery Farm,*
> *Little Laxlet,*
> *Burside.*
>
> *August 6th, 1933*
>
> *Dear Bettina,*
>
> *Remember when I told you, ages ago, that I wanted to be married and have children by the time I was 21 and none after that?*
> *Well, I think I've found the perfect man for a husband. His name is ~~Xver~~, ~~Zviar~~, Xviar (I hope I've spelt it right) and he is very nice, but his mother is a bit toffee nosed.*
> *It's the county show in two weeks. Please come and stay and you can look him over, your opinion is important.*

It's a bit crowded here in the farmhouse but there's room if you don't mind sharing with me.

John and Alfie will still be on their school holidays, I know that, but I've had a word with Hilda and she says she will be delighted to have them to stay with her.

Please say yes.

Love,

Ada

xxx

Stan took us to Little Laxlet in his van, excitement building within the boys, the nearer we were to arriving at the picturesque village. Gradually the urban landscape of neat houses with their neat front gardens changed to rolling fields and hedgerows. A heat haze rose from the road ahead and Stan joked that he hoped the tyres would not melt.

"Let me know if you smell burning rubber, boys," he laughed.

Hilda, sitting on her front step waiting, greeted us with open arms. She had been a big part of our lives when we had lived next door in Groat Cottage, and was clearly delighted to see us. The table, groaning under the weight of all the food she had prepared, was further indication.

Catching up with the village news, Hilda said, "I've made enquiries with Jim (Landlord of the Shoulder of Mutton pub and owner of Groat Cottage) and Herbert Flitch still has the tenancy next door but isn't living there. I still hear people coming and going, though, mostly at night,"

Stan and I exchanged a concerned look, but with a certain air of caution, so as not to worry Hilda.

"We will be popping over to Providence House before going to Rookery farm. How do you think they are managing?" I asked, anxious for Agatha and my grandparents.

"I don't know how that girl copes with them, but I gather Mrs Davis and her boys are helping. Did you know that all five Davis boys are going to join the police force? The older two already have."

Providence House nestled in its beautiful and still rather overgrown garden at the bottom of the grassy bank, sandstone walls gleaming in the afternoon sun, a cat sleepily observed us as we approached. Honeysuckle and roses tumbled over the walls, and swallows swirled into the eaves of the stone slab roof. In no way did the outside appearance belie the chaos within.

Inside, Grandfather continued to hoard all manner of mess. However, he seemed very pleased to see me, and welcomed Stan and the boys.

Agatha looked weary, but brightened up when I suggested she might enjoy a day out with us at the county show.

Grandmother persisted in her refusal to get out of bed, only agreeing to sit in her chair if bribed with a cigarette and a glass of sherry. I sighed inwardly at the squalid state this lovely house was in, but realised the difficulties Agatha was having with her, now very elderly, parents. Silently I gave thanks for Mrs Davis and her sons.

John and Alfie made themselves quite at home when we went to Rookery Farm, and enjoyed helping to feed the animals, bringing the cows in for milking, and collecting warm eggs from the hens. Wearing their wellington boots and carrying sticks they looked like the country boys they really were, enjoying their time on the farm and banter with Ada's brothers.

"How are we all going to get to the county show?" I asked Ada.

"Well, I'll be going in the horse box early, with me dad and Raven," she replied, smiling, as she always did while speaking of her beloved horse. "We need to be there early, to settle him and get ready for the show jumping. Everybody else will be going in the charabanc, our Molly has hired it for the day, and it seats twenty, so you'll be okay. There's quite a few from Little Laxlet booked on it."

Once in Ada's feather bed, our conversation turned to matters of the heart.

"I can't wait for you to meet Xavier," Ada gushed.

"I wouldn't rush into anything," was my cautionary response.

"Your Stan is lovely, do you think you'll be marrying him?"

"Doubt it," I responded. "We are becoming more like old friends these days."

"Did you know that at some family planning clinics, you can go for advice once you're engaged," Ada said.

"No, I did not know that," I said.

"Oh yes, I know a few girls who share an engagement ring, and they all go for advice wearing it – not all at the same time, of course, but tell them at the clinic that the wedding date is set," Ada affirmed.

"I don't think I'm ready to be married. After all, you and I are not even eighteen years old yet," I said.

"Well I am ready," was her response.

The county show was bustling, and full of all manner of country related activities. Agatha and Hilda enjoyed their day out, and Ada's brother, Watson, won first prize of a red rosette for his tup.

Xavier Brown was introduced to me by an excited Ada.

At first, I took his banal manner to be that of a shy person, but I soon became aware that this anodyne man in his early twenties would very quickly become boring for Ada, which would not bode well for their relationship. I found him uncomfortably polite and difficult to converse with.

His narrow-eyed mother and I were introduced, and as we shook hands, she looked me up and down commenting, "So, I'm given to understand that you are a town girl. It must be difficult for you to have an understanding of country life." I smiled sweetly at her, whilst inwardly grimacing and quickly making the decision not to relay my life story to her.

"I'm immensely proud of Xavier, such a good seat, sure to come away with a rosette today, He's an accountant, you know," said Mrs Brown, patting her tightly curled perm and puffing out her chest as she spoke.

"So clever my boy, always came top in everything at school, bit of a genius really, though I don't like to brag…" she went on and on and on!

"You must be proud of him," I responded whilst thinking – she's talking *shite*!

"I live in Burside with my wonderful Xavier and my other son."

"You have two sons, are they both here today?" was about all I could think of to say to this woman, whilst looking for an excuse to escape.

She declined to tell me about her other son, who possibly may also have been a genius but fortunately I saw Agatha in the distance and immediately extricated myself. I neither cared or had any interest in Mrs Brown's sons, but worryingly Ada seemed very taken with one of them.

Mrs Brown must have been rather disappointed, as Xavier did not win a rosette. However, Ada and Raven did win a rosette, and a silver cup, much to the joy of all from Little Laxlet, who cheered and clapped with vigour when Ada stepped forward to be presented.

John and Alfie enjoyed Ice Cream, lemonade, rides on the carousel, shuggy boats, bumper cars, helter-skelter and won a prize each on 'hook-a-duck'.

Agatha spent some time chatting to a lady spinning wool, found a stall selling lace making bobbins and thread, making several purchases.

Hilda met up with many old friends she hadn't seen in a while, proudly showing off John and Alfie and informing anyone who would listen that the boys would be staying with her tonight.

We all returned to Little Laxlet in the charabanc, singing 'Show Me The Way To Go Home' almost in unison, happily tired. Many comfort stops were made on the way back to the village for the men who hadn't been much further than the beer tent at the show.

The charabanc driver dropped me off at Rookery Farm gate and, walking across the stack yard to the house, I was troubled as to how I was going to express my thoughts regarding Xavier and his dreadful mother to Ada, knowing how enthusiastically she had earmarked him as husband material.

As it happened, there was no immediate worry, as Ada was fast asleep when I entered the bedroom, and did not stir as I climbed into bed.

10

Strange Goings On

Brushing down Raven with Ada the following morning, I felt nervous about the prospect of being honest with her regarding my opinion of Xavier. She looked glum, which was hard to understand, considering her success yesterday at the show. We brushed his black shiny coat in silence for a while whilst he munched away at his hay net.

"It's all off," she eventually said, her voice trembling with raw emotion.

"All off?" I echoed.

"That stuck up bitch Mrs Brown said she thought her Xavier should have won, and he, her precious son, had the bloody brass neck to agree with her, so I dumped him. I can't stand a bad loser."

I felt relieved at her self-assured, acceptance and I confirmed that she had made the right decision.

"There's something going on at Groat Cottage," I said, hoping to engage her in matters other than those of the heart.

"Going on … in what way *going on*?" was, as I'd hoped, her interested response.

"Comings and goings in the night, according to Hilda," I said.

"Sounds decidedly suspicious to me. are we going to investigate? Oh please tell me we are, I've always wanted to be a detective," Ada said.

"Yes, but it will need to be after dark – say about 10pm tonight," I said.

It was decided we would wear trousers and gloves as there may be some climbing involved. We would travel by bicycle – there were several in the barn.

My activity during the day was with John and Alfie, mostly looking for frogs in the pond at Providence House. Grandfather continued to refuse any help removing his hoard. This confirmed further to me that his need to have so much junk was a comfort to him for the loss of his three sons, and also having Grandmother as his main companion with her dementia. However, he did enjoy now being able to sit in his garden again since Stan had cleared it. Any thoughts I may have had of trying to over-rule him with his hoarding on the grounds of safety, I decided would be unworthy of me.

Leather on willow was the sound which drew myself and the boys to the village green. Simon Blackwood had organised an impromptu cricket match to which John and Alfie were invited. It gave me pleasure to observe the boys enjoying playing cricket with the other village children. Sitting on the warm, dry grass in the comforting shade of the beech tree, with Sophie, Simon's spaniel, I stitched some paper piecing in readiness for my quilt, making the day perfect.

On our gentle walk back to Hilda's, we picked brambles, supposedly for a pie, but the boys ate most of them. I left two boys, their faces bramble juice stained, with Hilda, who took the children into her arms as though they were her own.

"We picked you brambles for a pie," John said, offering Hilda a handful of brambles.

"Wonderful," she said. "With your brambles and my apples, we'll bake that pie for tea."

10pm saw Ada and me cycling from Rookery Farm on our mission to uncover evidence regarding 'the mystery goings on' Hilda had spoken about. Switching off the lights before we entered Little Laxlet, we left our bikes hidden behind a hedge, and walked over two small fields, behind the pub and allotments to the back gate of Groat Cottage.

Gently and quietly, I lifted the latch, and we crept into the yard. Thankfully there wasn't a full moon, and there were no signs of current occupancy. I signalled to Ada that I would shin up onto the wall, then open, with the aid of a pen knife, the window of the bedroom which used to be mine. She would keep watch, and hoot like an owl to warn me if needs be.

The window opened without much effort and made little noise. Then I was in the cottage, and in my old bedroom, which looked much as I had left it, but exceedingly dusty.

Venturing downstairs, I wondered if the treadle sewing machine would still be in the living room, and it was, alongside about 50–60 boxes of various sizes. Wearing gloves, and by the light of my torch, I could see the boxes were sealed and stamped, 'BRITISH ARMY SUPPLIES', some were marked 'HAZARDOUS – THIS WAY UP'.

I nearly jumped out of my skin when I felt someone behind me. It was Ada, who had quickly grown tired of keeping watch, and was curious as to what was going on. I was relieved to see she was still wearing her gloves. I signalled her to keep quiet, and then illuminated the boxes for her to see the stamps on the sides.

It was then we heard voices, and the sound of the back door being opened. We flew upstairs as quietly as possible, and squeezing together, we hid under my old bed, and listened as the sound of voices came up through the floorboards.

"Not much this time," a man's voice said.

The sound of footsteps on the stairs which then proceeded into the front bedroom.

"Ten boxes in 'ere." We heard the same voice again.

The door to the little bedroom opened, and the man came in. We could see his muddy boots and the lower legs of his mud spattered trousers as he walked across the room, stopping at the side of the bed.

"Only a couple of boxes in 'ere," he shouted, then left, closing the door behind him.

A different voice resounded throughout the cottage. "It's the big one next week, Tuesday after dark, so I'm told. 'Ere's those fags I told yer about. I've opened the box"

Silence then the sound of a match striking

"'E'de kill us if e knew we was nicking 'is fags," said a male voice.

"Yus right but I won't be tellin' 'im and if yu 'av 'alf a brain neither will you?" a voice replied.

Ada stifled a sneeze, and I shushed her, emphasising that silence was vital.

"Any idea what's on for the Tuesday trip?" said a voice.

"No idea. Only know it's big," was the reply.

"Did I 'ear im say 'ed done a recky?" questioned the man.

"Yeh, no probs. There's only a dopey old bat livin next door," the other man replied.

We waited under the bed, hardly daring to breathe, until we heard the sound of the back gate closing and the doors of the vehicle being slammed

Peeping out of the window I could not see the faces of the men clearly, just the tips of their cigarettes glowing in the dark as the drove away.

"Shall we have a look in the boxes?" Ada asked excitedly.

"No, not a good idea. Best not to risk it. They might come back. We need to leave now, very quietly and very quickly, and making sure the bedroom window is secure, and looking just as it was," I replied.

Back at the farm, in the safety of Ada's big bed, I swore her to absolute secrecy, stressing the danger of not being so; then I had to decide the best way forward. The only thing which meant more than life itself to Ada was Raven, her magnificent stallion.

"Now Ada," I said. "I shall be going to the police with this, in an anonymous capacity. It is *extremely* serious and could turn nasty, so please say absolutely nothing to anyone or you and Raven could be in danger."

I reassured Ada that so long as she kept quiet there would be no risk to either of them.

The boys and I returned to Ransington the following day and after dark I cycled to a telephone box, well away from Iona House.

Firstly, I made a 999 call to the police, and anonymously gave them the information, regarding the movement of stolen goods from the Army base, and where the goods were stored.

I then cycled to a different telephone box, contacted the army base, and asked to speak to the Commanding Officer, stressing urgency. Fortunately, he was in, and willing to accept an anonymous call. I mentioned that the army boxes could contain hazardous material, and that I had given the information to the police regarding further movement of stolen goods on the next Tuesday night. He asked me why I wished to remain anonymous.

I said, "Because I am frightened, Sir."

I then hung up the receiver, and left the telephone box as quickly as possible.

Following these calls, I then needed to wait patiently.

A telephone call from Hilda, using the telephone box on Little Laxlet village green, the following Wednesday morning informed me, in a very urgent and excitable voice that there had been a police raid on Groat Cottage.

"Bettina, pet, I'd just gone to bed last night when I heard a commotion next door. It was a police raid, and three men have been arrested and taken away. The army are there now, with more police, looking for fingerprints, I expect. I over-heard a policeman say something about stolen goods from the camp, and I caught a look at one of the men they arrest-ed, and he looked just like Herbert Flitch, in fact I'm sure it was him."

"Thank you Hilda for letting me know. Are you okay?"

"I am that pet, and thankful they've caught them. I knew something was going on. The police must have been watch-ing the place."

"Thank you again Hilda. I'll try to get over to see you before too long," was all I said.

It was eventually reported in the newspaper that the three men were now in custody for handling stolen goods from the army base were Herbert Flitch, Richard (Dicky) Pearson, and Malcolm May, (Mrs Flitch's boyfriend), who worked at the army camp and was the 'inside man'. All three had been charged, apprehended and were now awaiting trial.

Mrs Flitch had had a narrow escape from criminal charges related to possession of stolen property. This was due to the fact that the tenancy of Groat Cottage was still in my mother Louisa's name, although she had died two years before. The terms of the tenancy were informal, but as the rent had been paid on a regular basis, and often in advance, Jim, the land-lord, had not formalised a new agreement.

Needless to say, Mrs Flitch would no longer be welcome to live in Groat Cottage and I doubted she would show her face again in Little Laxlet.

11

Delicia

The gardens of Iona House were beginning to look and smell autumnal in the September of 1933. Cobwebbed shrubs and plants, shrouded in the filmy veil of morning mist, producing red, yellow and purple berries, mostly for the birds' winter diet.

John and Alfie had returned to school following their summer break and I was busy working in the office for Stan each weekday morning and sewing in the afternoon. The new quilt was now in the planning process and I had begun to enjoy gathering coloured fabrics with pretty floral patterns.

Claudette had enjoyed her second birthday at the end of August and Rory was now one year old. We had a joint tea party for them and although he enjoyed the fuss, I imagined that if he could actually hear us singing Happy Birthday it would be so much more fun for him.

Stan and I had made the mutual decision to no longer be boyfriend and girlfriend which suited me well, although I knew we would always be friends. I understood, from his mother, that Stan now had a new girlfriend and that Mrs Handyside did not care for her. I recall the word 'trollop' being used when the girlfriend was discussed and Stan's mother was convinced that 'the trollop' was only after his money!

I received a letter from great aunt Eliza Jane.

High Stones,
Gosforth
Newcastle upon Tyne

September 9th, 1933

My Dear Bettina,

What did I tell you about that Herbert Flitch, I knew he was up to no good. There has been quite a bit in the papers here and I think his trial will be before Christmas or in the New Year.

The reason for this letter is that I must delay my visit to Ransington this year as I'm expecting a visitor from America. She is the grand daughter of my dear friend Caroline and will be visiting Great Britain for several months. I shall be delighted if you could come and stay here for a few days to help to welcome her as she is about your age, perhaps a year or two older. Photography is her main hobby and she is interested in visiting our cathedrals, museums etc. Her name is Delicia Jennifer Van der Linden and she is due to arrive later in the month.

Please give my love to all at Iona House.

Your loving Aunt,

Eliza Jane.

p.s. I will send you the dates as soon as I have them.

Delicia Jennifer Van der Linden was travelling with The White Star Line from New York and was due to arrive in Liverpool on September 23rd.

A telegram was delivered to Great Aunt Eliza Jane,

In Liverpool.stop. Have met a Lord.stop.See you in three days.stop
Delicia Van der Linden.stop

Lord Algernon Ralph Grensom, the incredibly handsome, second son the the Marquess of Mear happened also to be travelling from New York to Liverpool on the White Star liner, 'The Britanic'. He found Delicia Jennifer charmingly charismatic, as she did him. The attraction between them developed into passion during the 6 day crossing, so much so, that on the first night they met, following an evening of dancing to the delightful orchestra, they spent a night of lustful desire in each others arms.

Neither of them went in for 'small talk' and as it was rather chilly on deck in September they invariably found themselves either in her luxury cabin or his,which was equally as luxurious.

One night their height of desire was such that it necessitated them climbing into a lifeboat. There, in the confined space and wrapped in Delicia's ocelot coat, they experienced the pleasure and wicked enjoyment of unbridled sex. What Delicia was unaware of was that Ralph had generously tipped a member of the White Star Line crew to make the lifeboat available for them, including pillows, a bottle of champagne and two glasses. Following their passionate lovemaking, and joyously sticky with love, they lay in each others arms, his fingers tracing her skin; watching the stars together, this was a night that would be etched into their memory forever.

During the crossing, in the comfort of either cabin, with sensual slowness they would undress each other whilst alternating kisses with sips of champagne. Ralph's tongue exploring her lips and sliding into her mouth. Her kisses reciprocated and, with his torso strong against her nakedness, fresh pleasures were aroused. They caressed and kissed each other's flesh until it tingled, both aching to be totally absorbed into the other, but wanting to wait, enjoying the love play until they could postpone no longer.

Sex for them was as natural as breathing – sometimes Delicia would take the initiative and straddle her most able lover whilst he caressed her breasts and nipples; maintaining a rhythm and momentum to bring utter and complete satisfaction to both.

When the liner docked in Liverpool they made the joint decision to spend two days and nights at the Adelphi Hotel to further extend their desire and longing for each other.

The Pear Belle Helen Dessert was a particular favourite of theirs and during their stay at the hotel, 'room service' would be asked to bring two with extra chocolate sauce, to their suite during the afternoon. The chocolate sauce was a prelude to more lovemaking. Delicia and Ralph, both lovers of chocolate second only to sex, enjoyed pouring it on, then licking the chocolate sauce off *every* part of each others anatomy, arousing fresh pleasures; delights too exquisite to describe...

A few days later.

Arriving at High Stones riding a Harley Davidson motor bike, wild curly hair the colour of mandarin oranges streaming about her, Delicia made her entrance. She had brought the motor bike from America, the panniers of which contained her cameras; the rest of her luggage would follow.

Great aunt Eliza Jane commented that, "The child is not as I expected, having been quietly brought up as a débutante at home; then finishing school in Switzerland. Her father is one of the richest men in America; made his fortune in construction, mainly the Transcontinental – Pacific railway."

"Gee you sure have a great house here and I just love a swimming pool – skinny dipping okay?" asked Delicia.

Aunt Eliza Jane, although broad minded, seemed visibly shocked.

"Well yes, I suppose so," she replied, "but please wait until Cedric and Cyril have left for work."

"I understand you are a keen photographer," I said.

"Sure am," was her reply, "thought I might take a few shots of those Abbeys and Cathedrals you have over here."

At dinner aunt Eliza Jane raised the topic of the telegram and the mention of the Lord whom Delicia had met on the liner.

Delicia explained that he was the second son of the Marquess of Mear so not in line to inherit the title but that she had been invited up to their Scottish estate for shooting in October, adding that he was the most handsome man she had ever seen.

"You know how some guys are just, well just, well you know… , blond hair, green eyes six foot three, six pack strong as an ox. Get the picture?" she sighed.

"He sounds most handsome," remarked great aunt Eliza.

'Not arf', I thought, whilst saying, "You must be looking forward to your trip to Scotland."

"We have and Abbey not far from here, at Hexham, if you would like to visit it," I suggested.

"Sure would – is it old?"

"12th century I believe," I replied.

"Great. I'll take loads of pictures. Don't suppose you guys have a dark room I could use for developing?"

Aunt Eliza Jane said she would enquire with Winnie and Gladys to see if a dark room could be made available at Gibbs.

John and Alfie were at school during the day and being looked after by Vera in the evenings. Stan and Bonny were sharing taking and collecting them from school so I knew I could relax and enjoy the next day or two with Delicia Jennifer Van der Linden.

12

Great Uncle

I found riding pillion on the Harley Davidson exhilarating, only closing my eyes when weaving through some busy traffic and overtaking a horse and cart on a blind bend.

Delicia rode with expeditious confidence, her flame coloured, long curly hair held in place by her goggles. We arrived in Hexham in what seemed to have been the speed of light, I then unclenched my teeth.

The Abbey, captivatingly beautiful in the Autumn sunshine, drew us in to explore. We did so, inside and out, to the accompaniment of the click,click of Delicia's camera. She seemed particularly interested in the stained glass windows, the crypt and the night stair.

As we toured the building she explained that her friend in New York, an editor of a magazine would pay good money for historical articles about Great Britain, especially with photographs.

This puzzled me as Great Aunt Eliza Jane had said that Delicia's father was one of the richest men in America – a multimillionaire.

I asked, "How is it you have a job as a photographer? I thought you were a débutante."

"Oh I am but my dad, he's such a tight-ass, real mean with those dollars of his, he's always made me earn my keep, even from being a little kid. My mom has to account for every penny she spends and I'm permanently hard up, hardly have a cent to my name."

I didn't quite know how to respond so I asked about Ralph whom she had met on the liner.

"That's the funny thing with dad, he'll pay big money if I marry into a title, and I mean BIG money," she answered, rolling her eyes. "My dowry is enormous, but I haven't told Ralph."

"Wow to the enormous dowry, very sensible for not mentioning it to Ralph" was my response.

"He heard, my dad that is, that the aristocracy over here are cash poor so his plan is to buy his way in."

"Do they know about Ralph?" I asked.

"Yes and no. Let's just say I'll keep them hanging on as long as poss," she replied with a wink.

"Well then my 'hard up' friend lunch is on me," I laughingly joked as we walked towards the tea shop.

We ordered lunch and the waitress serving us recognised me from my previous visit.

"Did you find Ford House?" she enquired.

"Yes thank you, I did and I met an old gentleman there; even though the house was empty and for sale."

"That'll be Tobias," the waitress said.

"Tobias, that's strange – my grandfather was Tobias and he lived there many years ago."

"Oh yes," she said, "there seems always to have been a Tobias living there, anyway for as long as I can remember."

Over our chicken salad I explained to Delicia about my previous strange visit to Ford House when Great Aunt Eliza Jane had had a disturbing and uncharacteristic reaction to seeing the old man.

"Can you remember how to get there?" Delicia asked.

"Yes, I think so."

"Okay then let's go buddy," she said.

A young woman with a small child in her arms opened the door of Ford House to us. I explained who I was and that we were looking for the old gentleman.

"That will be Tobias," she said, "he lives in the cottage through the woods. The gate is just round that corner of the house, follow the path and you will find him. Leave your motor cycle here if you want, it will be perfectly safe."

We followed the narrow woodland path and eventually found the cottage which was situated in a wild and wonderful garden overlooking open fields for as far as the eye could see.

Small and perfect I would consider to be a good description of this pretty cottage. Built in sandstone with pink roses tumbling over the porch, surrounded by flowers and the wonderful perfume of a late summer garden.

The old gentleman was absorbed in tending to a hive of bees but he looked up and at us through his bee-keepers veil as we drew near saying in a quiet voice, "I wondered if you might return. Please come in, Do you like honey?"

Inside the incredibly well furnished cottage, where a magnificent azalea plant took pride of place on the hall table, I explained that my aunt had thought he was my grandfather who had died 30 years earlier.

"Yes, I'm told that I look very much like my father, Tobias Pym," he said.

"Tobias Pym was your father!" I exclaimed, hoping that my jaw had not dropped.

"Yes but my surname is not Pym, you see my parents never married. I am Tobias Fisher, I imagine curiosity brought

– 87 –

you here, would you be interested to hear my story?"

Delicia and I both agreed we would be extremely interested to hear his story.

"My mother," Tobias said, "was a 13 year old orphan when she came to work as a maid for the first Mrs Pym around about 1870 I recall being told. Her name was Hannah Fisher and she had been living in a charity home for orphaned girls. Hannah had attended school up to the age of 12 years and could read and write so she was considered suitable for the position of kitchen maid at Ford House.

Initially she found the work hard though manageable, however because she could read and write, Mrs Pym promoted Hannah to the position house maid.

After about a year Mr Pym began to have, what mother described as, an obsession, with her, Hannah would have been about 14 years old. His wife was an invalid and spent much of her time at their Newcastle town house which was more convenient for hospital appointments I suppose."

"What did Tobias Pym do for a living?" Delicia asked.

"Import and export but import mostly. Mainly alcohol such as brandy and gin, fine wines and occasionally other goods such as silk, exquisite cloth and garments from the Orient.

When Tobias was in residence here at Ford House Hannah was his mistress, or 'wife', so he told her. He declared his love for her and that when she was of age he would divorce Mrs Pym and they would be properly married. In the event of Mrs Pym dying, and if Hannah was over 16 years, then then they would be married.

My mother was just 15 years old when I was born – over there in the attic bedroom in Ford House."

"A baby at aged 15 years. That can't have been easy for Hannah," was my comment.

"It wasn't easy for her," Tobias continued. "But Tobias Pym told Hannah that he was thrilled to have a son as he and the first Mrs Pym had no children. A vow was given by him to Hannah that he would always look after us. That was the reason he had this cottage built as our home – always with the promise of marriage when the first Mrs Pym died, following which we would move into the big house.

Hannah continued to work for Tobias Pym and progressed to the position of housekeeper. Keeping the house immaculate and dreaming of the day when she would become the second Mrs Pym and we would a live as a family in Ford House instead of Ford Cottage.

At 7 years of age I was sent to an exclusive school for boys where I received an excellent education all paid for by my father who was named as my benefactor on all documents.

When I was about 14 years old the first Mrs Pym died in Newcastle and Hannah, because she had been promised, began to prepare for her wedding.

Following the funeral Tobias had a discussion with mother and suggested that perhaps to marry too quickly after his wife's death might look disrespectful and to wait two years would be more appropriate.

You can imagine Hannah's disappointment having waited all those years to now have to wait for another two. She had hoped to have more children and become a 'respectable' woman and no longer a servant. However she had no choice but to agree.

I was away at school at the time but I gathered from what

the servants told me in my school holidays that Hannah soon perked up and began gathering her trousseau in preparation for her marriage to Tobias Pym. She made many of the garments herself which kept her busy and every morning she struck the previous days date off the calendar, counting down until her wedding; which Hannah expected to be two years following the death of the first Mrs Pym.

When the news came that Tobias had re-married one year after the death of his first wife it was an enormous blow for Hannah. The first she knew of it was when the butler brought in a newspaper containing a wedding photograph of Mr Pym with his new wife, Letticia Ann who, Bettina, I believe was your grandmother.

The shock was overwhelming for Hannah as you might imagine. But 'What doesn't kill you makes you stronger.' her words not mine. However I do believe that was the moment she became bitter and jealous – not surprising I suppose."

We both sat quietly, enraptured by this story and I did wonder if Delicia had plans to write a piece for her magazine editor friend in New York about Hannah.

Tobias offered us a cup tea, which he made, then he continued with the account of his mother in a most matter-of-fact manner.

"Your grandmother, Letticia Ann, was a radiant and beautiful young woman of about 20 years old which made for a huge age gap, as father was 50 years old at the time of their marriage. She did try to settle here but I gather, rather like the first Mrs Pym, her preference was for the town house in Newcastle.

Amazing dinner parties were held here, over at at Ford House, and Letticia Ann was a most glamorous hostess. I remember thinking how breathtakingly dazzling she looked and how her rubies and diamonds sparkled in the candlelight on the one occasion I saw her waiting to receive guests.

Hannah 'put on a good face' because Tobias was still paying for my education and this cottage was our home.

It became increasingly obvious that the new Mrs Pym, your grandmother, was not happy and after a few years stopped even visiting Ford House; her home now being in Newcastle. After some years she gave birth to two daughters, one of whom must have been your mother my dear, but they never came here not even to visit.

The dinner parties continued without her however, alcohol flowed in abundance, the guests now became all men rather than couples. Tobias provided entertainment in the form of gambling, destitute young girls and sometimes boys; always pretty and desperate to escape their situation in life. These youngsters were considered by Tobias Pym and his guests to have no future other than prostitution or crime so Tobias enabled the men, to use them as sexual play things. The dinner parties were no more than sexual orgies.

Mother tried to hide what was happening from me but, listening to the other servants provided me with a good idea of what was going on.

Tobias had, of course, now lost interest in Hannah completely as a partner, either inside or outside of marriage, the void in her life became filled with anger, hate and jealousy – not a healthy combination."

"What about you," I asked. "It can't have been easy for you living in such a situation."

"Me" Tobias replied, "When my education was complete I became a school master teaching Greek, Latin and maths, all wonderful subjects. Delicia my dear, your name intrigues me. Are you aware that it means delightful and is of Latin origin, not a name one hears often?"

Delicia said, "I'm glad you like my name, my father is Dutch and it is the name of his mother and grandmother."

Tobias then carried on with his story.

"The orgies continued, with children being brought by carriage to sexually satisfy the lusting of men, most of whom were considered to be 'pillars of the community'; both married and unmarried, most holding high office and stature in this area.

Hannah, when she realised that I was fully aware of the nature of these parties, stressed the importance of my silence telling me she was dealing with it and we did not want to lose our home.

I recall one particular night, which was unpleasant to say the least.

A young woman of about 16 years escaped and was hunted in these woods by men, one of whom had a dog.

We hid her in our attic and mother sprayed a strong herb solution all around the cottage to put the dog off the scent of the girl. We kept her hidden for a few days until Tobias Pym was away on business. The dray called to take the empty beer barrels to the railway station; they then went by train to the brewery in Newcastle. Dressed in my clothes, the girl was hidden in a marked half barrel which had some holes drilled in it for air. She travelled by dray then train to Newcastle where Hannah's brother unloaded the frightened child in the malting's yard.

"How did he know there would be a child in the barrel or that the dray-men would not roll the barrel?" I asked.

"None of this was ever spoken of officially nor was there ever anything in writing but the dray-men were 'in the know' and Hannah's brother knew to look for marked barrels."

"What happened to the girl?" Delicia asked.

"It was not unusual for mother to rescue a child and transport him or her to safety in that way. The girls were found work in the hotel trade, usually as chamber maids; the boys also worked in the hotels or on the market.

Following a particularly rowdy orgy Hannah expressed to me her disgust and loathing for Tobias Pym.

I understand the phrase 'tipping point' to be an apt description of the situation and, although she said nothing of it to me, I think that is when she made the decision to kill him."

"Kill Him!" Delicia and I gave unanimous and audible shriek.

"Yes, kill him. Bitterness is such a fruitless emotion and I could see melancholy in her eyes. She had always been an excellent cook and knew the dishes which Tobias Pym favoured.

Potted trout with Melba toast as a first course, followed by a large portion of steak and kidney pie accompanied by several glasses of the port wine to which he was especially partial, cooked and served by Hannah. On rising from the table Tobias Pym dropped to the floor with a heart attack. Mother had always had an interest in herbal concoctions so it is my belief that she poisoned him.

Then she calmly reached for a cream velvet cushion from the arm chair. That is the very same chair, there, over there in the corner. Hannah then pressed the cushion over his face until she was absolutely sure he was dead.

On removing the cushion there was a death mask imprint

in the velvet which she gently smoothed away. Plumping the cushion and carefully replacing it on the chair she then took from her pocket a swans down feather which she placed on Tobias's upper lip just to confirm he was not breathing. Hannah then summoned the butler and asked him to send word for the doctor to attend.

Immediately following removal of the body, most of the furniture from this cottage was replaced with furniture from Ford House. This was on Hannah's instruction and with help from the other servants. Valuable antiques so my friends tell me.

His last will and testament made an interesting document as he was bankrupt at the time of his death. Unsurprising I suppose as he was a gambler. From what the solicitor told me, the Newcastle town house belonged to your grandmother, and this cottage and garden was mine as he had made those arrangements long before he died. I remember that mother was quite 'put out' for a while to find that the cottage was in my name and not hers. We lived here together for several years until she died, never at peace, a broken woman.

I shall live here until my own demise as it is what I am used to. My bees need me and are very contented.

That is about all there is to tell you about Tobias Pym – caring father, gambler, philanderer and abuser of young children.

Delicia and I sat there somewhat stunned at such open and direct revelations from this quiet, gentle man.

"May I take some pictures of your yard and beehives Sir," Delicia asked.

"Of course you may and please call me Tobias, after all I am Bettina's great uncle.

Now Bettina if you would be kind enough to write down your full name and address in this book for me I shall then be able to send you a Christmas card."

Delicia was in the garden taking photographs of the hives and the cottage when we joined her. She took a photograph of Tobias tending his bees and one of him and I standing together beside a huge sunflower saying that she would send him a copy. We said our goodbyes and he insisted on giving each of us a jar of honey to take home.

Walking back along the woodland path and into the clearing where Ford House stood and where the motor cycle waited as we had left it, I said, "That was pretty interesting, looking back into my past with an uncle I didn't even know I had."

"Sure was," was her reply, "and did you see the size of those foxgloves in the yard! They've finished flowering now but the seed pods are fat to bursting"

The word digitalis sprang into my mind!

Returning to High Stones I showed Delicia the huge oil painting from the town house, now cleaned and hanging in the hall. We both agreed that Letticia Ann, my grandmother, had been a beautiful woman. With her two young children, Vera and Louisa, she looked so radiant and happy. However, one thing was different – the handsome groom who had been looking across at Letticia Ann so lovingly had been painted out of the picture!

13

The Car

Early November 1933 and a letter arrived from my aunt Agatha.

Providence House,
Little Laxlet.
November 1st, 1933

My Dear Bettina,

I'm writing early this year for your birthday to remind you of what your grandfather said about buying you a car. He has mentioned it to me on more than one occasion and I firmly believe he means what he says.
We would love to see more of you and the boys and with your own transport just think how much easier travelling would be for you.
Frank has been doing some research and a new Morris Minor car can be purchased for £100.
I have discussed this with dad and he says that is fine with him.
Mrs Davis is a Godsend and her youngest, Owen, is keeping the garden tidy for us.
I enclose a cheque for £150 just in case the car costs more.
Please keep in touch and let us know how you get on.
Love,
Agatha xxxx

I had to agree with Agatha that to own and drive my own car would certainly be a huge advantage for me, so in preparation I applied for a driving licence.

Stan, now infatuated and serious with his new girlfriend, meant we saw very little of each other and I made the decision not to consult him on the matter of buying a car.

Percy, our chauffeur/handyman was most helpful arranging with a friend of his, who owned a garage, for me to have a trial run in a new Morris Minor.

Percy accompanied me and he drove the car to a quiet road where he suggested I should have a try at driving. This I did and following a couple of 'jumpy' starts found the experience most enjoyable.

I purchased the car and Percy was kind enough to sit with me during my first few outings. He was a most patient instructor and gave me some sound advice regarding safety and the rules of the road.

Before long I became confident and was driving by myself and felt a surge of excitement at the prospect of the independence owning my own car would bring.

My relationship with Stan was now completely work orientated as his spare time was taken up with his new girl friend whose name I discovered was Phyllis; although still referred to as 'that trollop' by his mother.

I was pleased Stan was happy with his new love as I had been corresponding on a regular basis with Adam Rutherford whom I had met when on holiday at aunt Eliza Jane's. He was a final year student of politics, economics and philosophy at Durham University. In his latest letter to me he had invited me to partner him to the University Christmas Ball which would take place on Friday December 15th, 1933.

If I accepted he would arrange accommodation for us with his landlady in Durham where he was sure she would agree to me having the spare bedroom.

Of course I accepted by return post and immediately then went into a panic regarding what I should wear.

Bonny was helpful and we looked at various evening dresses both in magazines and also in the department store.

"Green is your colour," Mrs Scribbins stated over a cuppa one washday morning. "What with the red in yr 'air and them freckles you'll be a bobby dazzler in green."

Her daughter, Mabel, who now cleaned at Iona house two mornings each week, was in full agreement.

Dora happened to be visiting and on overhearing the conversation suggested that as it was to be a Christmas ball then red would be a suitable colour.

'Unlikely' I thought.

Vera wondered if cream might be appropriate and Mrs Handyside suggested blue.

Feeling confused I decided to buy a pattern and look at fabric.

With only a few weeks to go I bought a pattern for a full length, backless gown of a simple design, bias cut and figure hugging.

The emerald green satin slipped about and was rather difficult to work with, but Bonny helped with pinning and fitting and by the second week in December I had my dress for the ball.

With all of my birthday money I purchased a pair of small heeled white satin shoes which were then dyed to match my dress; silk stockings and new underwear completed my outfit. Vera lent me her gold clutch bag and fur cape. My jewellery would be the gold locket which contained a picture of mam; given to me by Vera and Angus the first Christmas I lived at Iona House.

I felt confident that I was now prepared for the ball and, leaving my beautiful dress on the tailors dummy covered by a sheet, I prepared for a pre Christmas visit to Little Laxlet. John and Alfie would be with me and we were all excited to demonstrate my driving and gratitude to grandfather and Agatha.

As we approached, Providence House looked wonderful in the pale winter sun and, I do believe my heart skipped a beat at the sight of it. Walking up the front path skirted with hellebores and sweet smelling daphne I could sense the warm welcome which awaited us from Agatha and grandfather. Poor grandmother no longer recognised me but always enjoyed the company of John and Alfie for a short while as she thought they were her own children.

The warmth and winter smell from the wood burning stove in the stable made comfortable accommodation for myself and the boys, who quickly climbed the hayloft ladder which is where they would be sleeping and I would spend the night in Agatha's huge four poster bed.

Grandfather was more than interested in the Morris Minor and said, "Come on then lass, ist tha takin me for a run?"

This I did; taking him for a 'run' to Rookery farm to call on the Smiths and place Vera's order for a turkey and a ham to be collected at Ransington market as usual on Christmas eve.

Ada was delighted to see us and whilst grandfather chatted with Mr Smith and the boys played on two old bikes they found in a barn, we caught up with the news.

I told Ada about going to the university ball with Adam and that Stan now had a new girlfriend called Phyllis.

She then exclaimed, "I'm that excited, I'm bursting to tell you – I'm courting!"

"Courting who?" I asked, wondering why she had never mentioned this in any of her letters.

"Well, almost courting," she said.

"What on earth do you mean, you are either courting or you are not courting," I said.

"Well I'm sure I will definitely be courting by Christmas, I've caught his eye," Ada said.

"Christmas is only three weeks away and you are talking in riddles," was my response. "Now calm down a bit and tell me what you mean."

"It's Emrys, Emrys Davis, oooh he is gorgeous. He's based at Burside police station and my friend Mary is on the switchboard so she knows his shifts and tells me when he's there," she said.

I asked, what I considered to be an obvious question, "Have you actually spoken to him or been on a date?"

"Yes and no, not yet," she replied, "but I'm working on it."

"Working on it!" I said, thinking 'Do I need to be worried'.

"Yes – it's called 'Purposeful Flirting', I read all about it in Womans' Weekly. It's all about getting him to notice me," Ada explained.

"And how do you propose to do that?" I asked.

"Well I found a wedding ring in Soot Lane, gold it is, and with help from Mary I took it to the Police Station when Emrys was there and handed it in to lost property. I looked into his eyes,dark blue and deep as the ocean they are, and he gazed back into mine," she said.

"Did he say anything?"

"Oh yes," Ada dreamily answered, "He said if it's not claimed in six months then it is yours. Now if that's not an omen then I don't know what is. I pop in quite regularly, supposedly to see Mary and when he walks by I flick my hair like this."

A demonstration of hair flicking followed.

"Has that worked," I asked.

"Well it would have except my kirby grip flew out and fell in his tea; next time I'll be less vigorous with my flicking."

I was about to tell my friend that I doubted that her 'purposeful flirting' was going to work when she announced that her next plan was to persuade Mary to hang mistletoe in the back office at the police station ready for Christmas and, when taking in mince pies for the policemen, Ada was sure Emrys would sweep her up in his arms and they would kiss passionately under it.

I did try to tell her that I thought her plan was crazy and smacked of desperation but she just sat there with an abstracted gaze, or what mam would have described as a 'daft look' on her face.

She must have then decided to close off the conversation regarding her plans as I, obviously, was not being supportive and said, "Okay then enough about me, tell me about this Adam you're always going on about in your letters. He sounds luscious."

I told Ada that Adam had invited me to the Christmas ball and that my dress was made and that I would be staying with him in Durham at his landlady's house.

"I've never been to a proper ball," Ada remarked. "Will you be sleeping with him at his landlady's house."

"I can assure you I will not be sleeping with him although I'm very excited about dancing with him, he is a wonderful dancer," I replied.

"Tell me about the dress then," she said, and I could tell she was disappointed that it didn't look as though we would be talking about sex.

We talked about the dress and I told her that I was unsure about wearing make-up and how to wear my long hair for the ball.

"Well do you know what I think," she said, "I think you will go to bed with Adam, he sounds gorgeous, I know I would – well not with Adam but with Emrys, my gorgeous Emrys. It's as much as I can do to keep my hands off him and I can just tell by the beguiling look in his eyes that he would be wonderful to fuck with. I read that in a magazine as well, 'beguiling' not the fuck bit."

I wished my friend well and hoped that she would not continue her quest in 'purposeful flirting' for too long.

"See you Christmas Eve at the market we both said and she added, "You just never know I might have news for you and will you be my bridesmaid?"

"Of course I will, but don't you think it would be a good idea to wait at least until you've been on a date with him before planning the wedding," was my laughing response.

14

The Telephone Box

Excitement woke me at 6am on the morning of Thursday December 14th, 1933 and for a moment I couldn't think why. Then quickly I realised that tomorrow was to be the day of the ball and to-day would be my preparation day.

I had already purchased and wrapped all the Christmas gifts for family and friends, including two new bicycles; one each for John and Alfie, now hidden in Percy's flat until Christmas. I had been able to buy the bikes from the remainder of the money that grandfather had sent me for my car.

Today was to be a day when I would wash my long hair then rinse it with collected rain water into which I would squeeze the juice of half a lemon. I would then try different hairstyles to see which would work best with my outfit for the ball – Bonny would help pinning my hair up and then assist me in my decision making. As well as the clutch bag and fur cape Vera had also lent me two gold hair slides.

With help from Stan's girlfriend Phyllis who was not a trollop at all, but an assistant on the cosmetics counter at the department store, I followed her advice regarding my hazel eye colour and purchased some foundation, face powder, an eye pencil, mascara and a lipstick. Today was to be a full dress rehearsal with help from Bonny, Vera, Mrs Scribbins and her daughter Mabel, who had asked particularly if she could see me wearing the complete outfit for going to the ball.

With wet hair I climbed the spiral staircase up into the beautiful tower room to look again at my dress which, if I say so myself, had turned out spectacularly well. As the sheet slid from the tailors dummy I gazed at my fabulous emerald green satin evening gown and loved it. The thought of Adam holding me close whilst dancing gave me a feeling of such excitement I could hear my heart beating in my chest.

Dawn was just breaking when I took my dad's war medal from its hiding place and, looking out over Ransington, I watched the gas street-lamps being extinguished at the start of the new day. I held Dad's medal for a few minutes wishing that he and mam were here to share my happiness which I knew was not possible; but just thinking of them calmed me.

At 8am I opened the front door to find a policeman standing there.

"Miss Bettina Dawson?" he asked.

"Yes that's me," I replied. "Is something wrong?"

"I'm afraid so miss, there's a fire at Providence House, Little Laxlet and I've been asked to give you that information."

"A fire … a fire …" I repeated, feeling slightly idiotic and nauseous with shock. "How serious, is anyone hurt?"

"I don't know any details miss, the fire brigade are at the property now. That's all I know."

I gave Vera the awful news and she immediately offered to look after the boys so that I could go to Little Laxlet.

By 9:30 am I was standing in the village looking in horror at the smouldering remains of what had been Providence House.

The firemen were still spraying and dampening the charred building which now only had half a roof. A policeman, whom

I recognised as Emrys, stood at the side entrance gate and informed me that it would be unsafe to go any closer as it was feared the building might collapse.

"Emrys," I asked. "Grandfather and Granny …"

I couldn't finish my question as his solemn expression held the answer.

"Agatha is safe though," he said. "She's over with Hilda. If you go to her I'm sure she will be pleased to see you."

Agatha, although safe, was almost incoherent with her explanation of the mornings events. From what I could gather, as the previous day had been a Wednesday and the chemist shop was closed for half day, Frank had been for her usual visit. The afternoon was quite dark and cold so they went to bed in the stable and fell asleep; waking at about 10pm. Frank then left as she had to cycle back to Burside ready for work the following day and Agatha went into the house to check on grandad and granny. They were both fast asleep in bed and all the oil lamps and candles were out so Agatha decided that, as the four poster bed in the stable would still be warm, she would sleep there for the night.

"The first I knew," she said, "was hearing a lot of banging, hissing and shouting. The firemen looked shocked and amazed when I walked out of the stable wearing only my nightdress and boots. They quickly brought me over here to Hilda's. It was Bryn, Bryn Davis who first saw the fire, on his way home from night shift. He ran to the phone box and alerted the fire brigade."

Agatha looked very small and afraid, sitting there in Hilda's arm chair wrapped in a blanket, bare foot and grimy- but alive!

"What do you want to do?" Hilda asked me "You are

both welcome to stay here , I'll go and fetch some clothes for Agatha then we shall have some breakfast."

Close to allowing the horror of the event to take control of my emotions I realised that I must stay strong for my aunt Agatha.

"Will you be okay with Hilda whilst I go and telephone Adam to put him in the picture and tell him that I now can't go to the Christmas Ball."

She nodded and I walked along to the telephone box on the village green. Providence House looked forlorn and broken as I passed. The firemen were continuing to spray water in through the upstairs windows.

I telephoned the university and spoke to a porter in the porters' lodge.

"Sorry miss, but the students have all gone home for Christmas."

Not having an address for Adam, other than his digs where I knew there was no telephone, I telephoned Vera and updated her with the news regarding the fire and that Agatha was safe.

"Bring Agatha here, she can stay with us until things are sorted out. I'll try to get a message to Adam for you," Vera said.

At about 2pm Hilda happened to be peeping out of the net curtains at her front window when a shiny black Humber limousine drew up outside the cottage. A handsome young man in chauffeurs uniform opened the rear door and a distinguished well dressed, elderly lady wearing five strands of pearls and a toque hat with ostrich feather emerged.

The commentary from Hilda ran, "Oh what a big car, it must be someone very posh and important – Oh my God it's the Queen herself. She's coming to the door."

We opened the front door to aunt Eliza Jane looking more like Queen Mary than I ever thought possible, so it had been easy for Hilda to make the mistake.

Without saying a word my aunt took me into her arms and embraced me, whispering how sorry she was and that I would find ways from within to deal with the situation. From that moment I felt my strength returning and knew I would cope.

Hilda just stood rooted to the spot, looking so amazed that I really think she thought my aunt was Queen Mary and in her cottage; that or she was dreaming.

I introduced them and they then recalled meeting many years earlier at my parents wedding.

Adam parked the limousine on the village green. When he joined us he carried a suitcase containing clothing from Winnie and Gladys for Agatha and a box containing one of aunt Eliza's orange cakes. Hilda made a cup of tea and I noticed that the best china tea service was now in use and that my aunt was offered the most comfortable chair in the room.

We discussed Vera's invitation for Agatha to stay at Iona House but Agatha said, "I can't go and leave mother and dad in the house over there, I just can't."

Adam had spoken to the firemen and they had told him that the property was too dangerous to enter at the moment but later in the day it might be possible.

"Now there is no way I wish to interfere, but would you girls like me to make the funeral arrangements for you? Being in the business I have good contacts, even as far away from Newcastle as this, we all know each other. I won't do anything without discussing it with you first," great aunt asked.

We both agreed it would be a good idea.

Later in the afternoon Bryn Davis called and told us that the bodies of my grandparents had been located and would be moved from the house in about half an hour. Providence House would then be boarded up and a 'DANGER – KEEP OUT' notice put in place on the front entrance. He suggested closing the curtains to spare Agatha further upset.

Just before 5pm Aunt Eliza Jane said, "We will have to leave in about an hour Bettina. I'm sure Vera would appreciate a phone call to let her know what's happening and that you and Agatha will be staying with Hilda tonight. It's dark out there so Adam will accompany you – the fresh air will be good."

I was pleased my aunt was there as I seemed unable to think straight.

As we walked Adam held my hand, there was an ease between us, holding hands in the darkness of the late afternoon.

Adam spoke first, "Don't worry about the ball Bettina. Naturally I'm disappointed but it can't be helped. There will be other balls."

"I'm so sorry Adam," was all I could think of to say.

Providence House looked pitiful as we passed, roof half caved-in, boarded-up and the acrid smell of fire hanging in the air.

Inside the telephone box with Adam beside me I spoke to Vera and she told me the boys were fine and she would expect Agatha and me in the morning.

Adam brushed a tendril of lemon rinsed hair from my face and I turned and looked into his brown eyes noticing, for the first time, how long and thick his eye-lashes were. A lock of his dark brown hair fell forward onto his forehead.

His arms gently encircled my waist and I found my hands sliding up to his shoulders then my fingers entwined behind his neck.

Our eyes locked, not a word was spoken as his soft, gentle mouth kissed mine, my response was to press my lips to his, closing my eyes – when in that moment the world stood still.

We stayed in a close embrace inside the telephone box for a while, me wrapped inside his coat the feeling of which, for a few minutes, assuaged my emotional pain. I then slid my arms around his waist feeling the tactile warmth of his woollen sweater and the comfort of his smell.

Tears welled up, first stinging my eyes then running down my cheeks which he gently wiped away before our lips met again in a delicious lingering kiss.

Holding me close I sobbed into his navy guernsey sweater making a very wet patch on his chest and hoping the wool wouldn't shrink.

A large white, freshly laundered handkerchief dried the tears, now dripping off my chin, whilst Adam joked that he always carried a large handkerchief just in case he stumbled across a weeping damsel in need of tear mopping.

We laughed for a moment, then he commented that he hoped folk wouldn't think that he had made me cry.

I knew my eyes would now be red and swollen, which is not a good look, but he tilted my face to his and gently kissed my eyes, the tip of my nose and then my lips.

We then, slowly, re-traced our steps back to Hilda's cottage and I realised that my world had changed in more ways than one and probably forever.

15

Stunning News

The time following the fire had been sad and difficult for both myself and Agatha. Vera and Angus made Agatha welcome and Frank had been to visit several times, bringing a lace pillow and bobbins from the stable/studio at Providence House.

Angus had asked me if I would like to accompany him to the Christmas poultry market an idea to which Agatha readily agreed saying, "It will do you good Bettina to get out, you might meet Ada who is bound to cheer you up."

On Christmas Eve I left with Angus at 7am, as was becoming the tradition, for the market where we collected the turkey and ham from Mr Smith.

Sitting in the van with Ada with our hot, steaming cups of tea Ada said, "It's ever so sad about your grandad and granny."

"It is, and we can't arrange the funeral until after the inquest, it could be January now," I said.

"How's Agatha bearing up?"

"Okay I suppose, under the circumstances. Her friend Frank came over to visit and brought her lace pillow, bobbins and thread so she is making her lace again."

"What about you?" Ada asked, in what for her was a most empathetic manner.

"Me, oh I'm okay I suppose, but Providence House is a

mess," I replied.

"I know, I passed it the other day – pitiful it looks. I don't suppose you went to the ball?" she said.

"No, but Adam says there will be others."

"Ooo – is *that* what Adam says? Sounds serious to me. Is it serious?" Ada asked.

"I think so, well it might be, although he's gone home for Christmas and I'm a bit busy right now with everything that's been going on. What about you?" I asked, hoping to be cheered up.

"Well I've applied for a clerical job at the police station in Burside. Had an interview yesterday."

"Clerical," I commented, thinking that clerical was not really Ada.

"Yes filing and such, I'm good at my alphabet and I'm hoping to grow into the role. That's what I told Miss Dent, she was the woman who interviewed me. Grow into the role; I'd read that in a magazine"

"What's was it like, the interview?" I asked.

"It was fine, except for the last bit," Ada said.

"Why what happened?" I said.

"She asked if I had any questions and I said no except when would I hear from her and thank you for the opportunity of an interview. It was then I smelt singeing."

"Singeing, how come?" I asked.

"I was sitting beside the gas fire and my best wool skirt was beginning to singe. Miss Dent had smelt it as well and apologised for the small room and having to sit so close to the fire. Apparently the usual interview room was being used for a very important meeting."

"Is your skirt ruined?" I asked.

"No, but she looked really embarrassed did Miss Dent and I have the feeling the job is mine," Ada said.

"Any romance," I asked, wondering if the 'purposeful flirting' had worked and if Emrys had asked Ada out for a date.

"Unfortunately no, but different policemen are posted to our station for training so once I'm a clerk there it will be just fine," she answered with confidence.

"However," Ada continued with a twinkle in her eye, "I have been out on a date and I sort of do have a boyfriend. It's Bernard, you know Bernard from the butchers."

"What was the date like," I asked, not having a clue who Bernard was.

"Talk about a disaster. First he suggested we should go for a walk. A walk in December, I thought bugger that, so I said to him you must be joking, no I won't go for a walk but I will go for a meal. His face didn't even flicker, he just said okay."

"Where did you go?" I asked.

"The White Hart, very la-de-dah it was. Proper menu, silver service. I can remember thinking as we enjoyed roast beef and red wine, I hope he isn't expecting me to pay for myself because if he is I'll dump him straight away. The food was lovely, I had a meringue for pudding but Bernard was soooo boring," she added, rolling her eyes.

"Collects stamps he does, bloody stamps, it was as much as I could do to stifle a yawn."

"Did he expect you to pay for yourself?" I said.

"Oh no, he coughed up the cash no bother, then we went for a walk," she answered.

"I thought you said no to a walk," I said.

"Well it was a short walk. A walk to the butchers shop. Bernard had the key and reckoned he had a bottle of brandy. Invited me in for a nightcap," Ada said.

"Brandy, do you even like brandy?" I asked.

"It was gorgeous – special reserve, I had a second one then we started to snog. Boring as hell he was with his stamps but what a brilliant shag we had on the floor under the counter. People were walking past but they couldn't see us in the dark, well I don't think they could. That big advertising plaster pig covers most of the window."

"So is he your boyfriend now, this Bernard?" I enquired.

"Oh no, although he might think he is. We meet up now and then for a shag and he always brings me a pound of sausages. Porkies he calls them," Ada said in a most matter of fact manner.

"Pork sausages – that's a strange present," I said.

"If you call that strange then you should see what he gets up to with his very own porkie – fucking fantastic it is!" she exclaimed.

"I hope you are taking precautions not to get pregnant," I said, wearing what I considered to be my sensible face.

"Rubber johnny that's the solution," she said.

"Porkies and rubber johnnies," I was flabbergasted but, as usual, we were both creased up with laughter when Uncle Angus tapped on the van window and it was time to leave.

"Bye bye Bettina, see you in the New Year."

"Bye Ada, have a Happy Christmas."

"You always have a good laugh when you see Ada," Angus remarked.

"That's true," I replied, declining to offer details of our conversation.

The result of the inquest was accidental death for both grandfather and grandmother. It was thought, following an investigation by the police and fire officers, a candle had set fire to some of the rubbish which was hoarded in the kitchen; that was where the fire had started and that is where the body of my grandfather had been found.

Agatha and I both received identical letters in early January, 1934.

SNODGRASS AND SNODGRASS – SOLICITORS

6 Hempside Lane
Burside.

January 3rd, 1934

Dear Miss Dawson,

Please accept my condolences on the deaths of Mr and Mrs Dawson. I understand that their funeral is to be on Tuesday January 9th, 1934 at 10 am and I am hoping to be there. An appointment has been arranged for you to attend this office at 3pm the following day to discuss matters which may be of benefit to you.
If you find this date and time inconvenient please contact my secretary to rearrange.
Yours faithfully,
Edward Snodgrass.

Sitting in Mr Snodgrass's rather formidable office Agatha and I did not quite know what to expect, never having attended a will reading before.

Mr Snodgrass began to read the wills.

The contents of which stated that Agatha and I were joint beneficiaries and would equally inherit half of her parents, my grandparents, estate which we did not anticipate being very much at all. They had let their farm go, the house was a burnt out shell and grandfather constantly reminded us that he was only a poor farmer.

Mr Snodgrass continued:-

Willow Wood Farm, consisting of farm house, barns, outbuildings, a cottage and 850 acres of land, currently tenanted – the tenancy to run for 4 more years.

Providence House, currently in a state of disrepair due to fire damage could be fully renovated as all insurance premiums are paid up to date.

Bank Holdings in savings accounts totalling £7,256 plus shares and investments.

Clemantine Dawson's jewellery – currently in a safe box in the bank due to her forgetfulness.

We both sat on the big wooden chairs feeling absolutely astonished.

Mr Snodgrass asked if we would like him to contact the insurance company on our behalf and we agreed.

He also told us that there would be a time lag whilst waiting for probate to clear but he would keep us informed.

Driving back to Iona House we were both stunned at the size of our inheritance and the responsibility which went with it.

"I had absolutely no idea they had so much," I said to Agatha.

"So much for being a 'poor old farmer'," she replied.

16

The Trial

On a Tuesday morning, later in January 1934, two armed police officers stood either side of the marbled entrance to the assize court.

I sat for part of most days, in the public gallery, to witness the trial of Herbert Flitch, Dickie Pearson and Malcolm May. (Lucrettia Flitch's boyfriend).

Judge Ian Mcleod recused participation in the trial, as Herbert Flitch's biological daughter was now Ian's niece by adoption, creating a conflict of interest.

Judge Whiteman, an assize judge, not renowned for leniency, would be taking the trial.

Lucrettia Flitch was also there, looking daggers at me from several seats away.

On the day of sentencing Ada and Agatha accompanied me and we sat side by side.

All three prisoners had been found guilty of the charge of handling stolen goods from the army camp, mostly cigarettes. However, the stolen items which increased the seriousness of the case was that some of the boxes had contained explosives and guns with boxes of ammunition – *side arms* the Judge referred to them as.

The cigarettes had been for Herbert and Dickie to sell on the market. The guns were destined for a notorious gang known as, 'The River Street Boys'. This gang were feared in the North East of England, working as they did extracting extortionate amounts of protection money from the owners of night clubs and bars, using brutality and fear when and where they saw fit. Rumour had it that the gang had links with gangsters as far afield as Birmingham and London.

One reason for the length of time the case had taken to come to trial was that Malcolm May had turned King's Evidence, giving information to the police regarding the River Street Gang. This had lead to arrests of gang members who were now in custody awaiting trial at a future date. He had done this in the hope of a more lenient sentence, which had been indicated, if not promised, when he was interviewed by the detectives.

As the stolen goods had been stored in a property to which he was the key holder, Herbert Flitch received a custodial sentence of 10 years.

Dickie Pearson received 5 years.

Malcolm May 2 years.

Lucrettia Flitch screamed, a scream both blood curdling and theatrical, as Herbert was taken down to begin serving his sentence.

We were leaving the Court when she raised her furled umbrella and, shaking it in my face, shouted at me in a distraught manner, her eyes stormy with hate: *"You are behind this Betty Dawson, I don't know how but I just know you are."*

I flicked a look across to Agatha and Ada indicating, 'Say nothing.'

Back in the safety of the Iona House kitchen I sat with Ada, each of us with a comforting cup of tea. I once again stressed to her the importance of not discussing the case with ANYONE. Especially now that we knew the connection to The River Street Boys' gang. If they found out that it was us who had made the discovery of the stolen goods and that I'd shopped them to the army and police then that would put us and our loved ones in danger. Ada assured me that she understood the gravity of the situation, and I truly believe she did.

A few days later in February Agatha said, "I've been in touch with Jim at The Shoulder of Mutton and he has agreed to me renting Groat Cottage."

I'd been aware for some time that Agatha was becoming restless and missing Frank, so I had to agree that this was probably the ideal solution for her, whilst Providence House was being rebuilt.

"Jim is having the cottage redecorated and is lighting the fire daily to air the place out," Agatha said.

"We will need to consult with an architect regarding the plans we have for Providence House," I said.

Agatha and I had spent many hours discussing the rebuild and both agreed that it would be a perfect opportunity to install electricity and have both a bathroom and flushing toilet upstairs, and downstairs a flushing toilet in the boot-room; both rooms to have hot and cold running water. In spite of the tragic circumstances which had lead to us owning the property we became quite excited and animated. Even discussing the possibility of having an extension to the rear of the property which we would call the orangery.

On February 14th, 1934 I received an anonymous Valentines card. Although it was unsigned the post mark read Durham which was a good clue that Adam had sent it. Later the same day he telephoned and invited me to visit him in Durham.

I thanked him for the card and we joked about how I knew it was from him.

Vera offered to look after John and Alfie and a two day visit was arranged for the beginning of March.

March 17th, and the city of Durham put on her 'pretty face' for me that weekend. As we strolled by the river Wear daffodils danced in the chilly breeze whilst primroses raised their faces to the weak rays of spring sunshine.

Out of the cold North East wind and into the quiet peace and shelter of the Cathedral we sat for a moment drinking in the magnificence of the building and just happy to be spending time together.

Adam already knew a great deal about me and my family circumstances but there in the tranquil atmosphere, I began to learn more about him.

He was from a mining family, living in the village of Denstag in county Durham. His father and two brothers were all pitmen and he had no sisters.

"Denstag, that sounds familiar to me. I think it could be a village I went to with my aunt to meet the quilting ladies."

"Could well be," replied Adam. "My mam quilts a bit and so does my cousin Jenny. Jenny makes fantastic quilts"

I wondered if Jenny was the same quilter who had been so helpful to me on my visit.

"Perhaps you would like to visit again, with me this time," he asked.

"I would, I really, really would," was my reply.

For tea, we sat in the market square eating fish and chips from the paper, followed by a visit to the cinema. The main picture was *The Thin Man* – a detective comedy. The Pathe News showed a film of the boat race and told us that Cambridge had won.

Walking back to Adam's digs he told me that following his finals in a couple of months he would be taking a job he had been offered with a national newspaper. The job was as personal assistant to a reporter and would be for six to eight weeks.

"That sounds interesting," I said. "Where will you be based?"

"Ah well," he replied, "I'll be going abroad to Europe; France and Germany mainly."

A sensation of anxious disquiet engulfed me as I'd heard of riots in Paris and that Chancellor Hitler in Germany was becoming even more extreme in his ideas regarding those who did not fit in to his ideals of an Aryan race.

Sensing my concern Adam reassured me by joking that he would be fine and said, "The pay is good, I speak both French and German and I won't have to dance with any ladies."

We kissed gently as if to seal the deal, I whispered "No dancing with ladies and come back safe."

We took our time strolling back but all too soon we were at the digs where Mrs Beason, Adam's landlady, had kindly put a hot water bottle in my bed in the spare room.

At my bedroom door we lingered in a soft and tender embrace, our bodies close and our arms entwined. His kiss which followed was not soft, but held a fire and passion which I returned in equal measure.

Then Mrs Beason coughed and we heard the click of her light being switched on.

"Is that you Adam pet?" she called.

"It is," he replied.

"Good night then, sleep well. I might get up just now and make a cup of tea," she said.

Slightly embarrassed and suddenly shy Adam said, "Would you like to use the bathroom first?"

I answered that I would, smiling and thinking how disappointed Ada would be that I would be sleeping alone.

The following morning Mrs Beason, wearing steel curlers, hair net and wrap around pinny over her dress, made us a substantial breakfast, following which we walked over the cobbles, window shopping and hearing the bells of the Cathedral ringing out.

A flight of fancy to hire a boat for an hour seemed the most natural thing to do and one which I found incredibly romantic. Listening to the oar blades dipping into the water, viewing the city from the river, and locking eyes with Adam, when safe to do so, as we drifted along. I felt emotions I couldn't put a name to, I only knew it was blissful.

Back on dry land and knowing I must leave for home soon and our lovely romantic weekend would end was tearing me apart. When the time came I could hardly bear it, so special had been our time together.

We held hands, then embraced each other tightly. My arms slid around his neck then my fingers gently tangled in his hair, whilst he held the back of my head; our lips gently crushing together in a long, lingering goodbye kiss.

"Thank you, it's been wonderful," I said in my most polite voice.

"Drive carefully now," was his response.

"Good luck with your exams," I said.

"Keep in touch," he called as he waved goodbye.

One month following the sentencing of Herbert Flitch,

Dickie Pearson and Malcolm May, the newspapers reported that Malcolm May had been discovered dead in his cell.

A letter from Ada, who now worked at Burside police station,and had 'inside information' told me that May's throat had been cut from ear to ear and the weapon had not been found.

In her letter she stressed to me the importance of never telling a living soul that we had discovered the boxes; a fact about which I needed no reminding.

17

The Morgan

Needles of rain pounded my little Morris car as we splashed our way to the bank that April afternoon. I noticed, and narrowly avoided, a small dog which was running up to people in the car parking area and trying to climb into their cars.

When I returned to the car from the bank the dog was still there and as I opened my car door it jumped in.

As much as I asked it to get out it refused.

I got into the car, the dog licked my hand.

I got out of the car. The dog jumped out.

Then, opening the car door as little as possible, I attempted to squeeze back in without the dog. This was a total failure as the dog was too quick for me and obviously thought, following several unsuccessful attempts on my part, that this was some kind of game.

'What is my plan B' I thought! 'Take it to a police station – problem solved.'

The little dog seemed perfectly happy sitting in the passenger seat but I knew that the police station was in a heavy traffic area and I did not have a lead.

"Now sit there and be good," I said to the dog who had a look of Bulls-Eye from Oliver. "I'm going back into the bank to see if they have a length of string."

She yapped in response, gave me a quizzical glance, turned

around a couple of times then settled back on the passenger seat.

The police station were not accepting lost dogs but gave her a drink of water and me the telephone number of the dog pound.

"That's a pip-squeak of a dog you've got there if ever I saw one," Percy said as we drove into the Iona House garage. "Could be a Jack Russell or a Staffy or a bit of both."

"I'm going to phone the dog pound straight away, she must be *some*one's pet," I said, heading for the house. "Please would you watch her for me?"

The dog pound had had no enquiries regarding a dog of her description and they were full.

Could I look after it, they had asked? Then if anyone enquired they'd be sure to put them in touch.

Percy and Pip were sharing a ham sandwich when I returned to the garage and the dog looked very settled on an old army blanket.

Vera said the dog could stay until the rightful owner claimed her so long as I looked after her.

John and Alfie loved Pip immediately, throwing the ball and taking her for walks in the park. I was somewhat more cautious about introducing the dog to Claudette and Rory as they were so young but they both took to her straight away and she to them.

In the conservatory at Iona House stood a huge bronze pot, rumour had it that it had come from China and that it was very old, possibly hundreds of years.

Knocking against the pot caused it to ring and vibrate which became a game for the children. Claudette would bang the pot with a stick and Rory would put his face and ear against the metal to feel the vibrations. This was a game they both loved and soon Pip was part of the game; her role was to fetch the thrown stick for Claudette to hit the pot. I understood that this Chinese bronze pot was valuable but Angus and Vera encouraged the game as it gave Rory a sense of sound.

No one claimed Pip so she now became part of the family. Sleeping in my bedroom at night and spending time in the tower room with me whilst I was working or sewing.

Of course she never refused a walk in the park or a ride in the car.

Rock Craig Castle,
Scotland.

April 12th, 1934

Dear Bettina,

Ralph and I are now engaged to be married. My parents are due to arrive in Scotland in a few weeks to discuss the wedding with his family.

Ralph is in Finland on estate business; timber negotiation to be exact. His older brother, Quentin, is supposed to be in charge of estate management but spends pretty much all of his time at the London house with his new lady. She is called Arjana Zabala and is a model or actress or both – not sure which.
He has fallen for her BIG TIME so we rarely see him here in Scotland. They seem to enjoy living in the fast lane – night clubs, cocktail parties etc.
My friend who edits the American magazine, I think I told you about her, would like me to do a story, with photographs, about York.

Would you be available to accompany me next week?
Please telephone your reply as the post can take for ever to
arrive here in the highlands.
Love,

Delicia xxx

April 19th, 1934

A loud hiss of steam, the clanking of couplings and we were aboard the train now bound for York.

The Minster was the main focus of Delicia's attention, she used a whole roll of film taking many shots. We then moved on to the ancient city walls and then to the river.

"I only have one roll of film left, shall we find The Shambles?" she asked.

We were both fascinated with the historical architecture where, I understood, that in some properties it was possible to shake hands with a neighbour across the street, so close were they.

We had discussed on our journey the possibility of buying a dinner gong for Rory. Knowing how much he enjoyed the vibration from the bronze pot then perhaps a dinner gong might have a different vibration for him, which he might enjoy.

"Gee the antique shops are real cute," Delicia said whilst clicking away with her Kodak Junior 620 folding camera – or 'portable, out and about model' she called it.

"Look!" I said, spotting a brass dinner gong in a shop window. Moving closer I also noticed a Christopher Dresser jardinière and stand identical to the one stolen from Ian and Dora's in the robbery. I quickly and quietly told Delicia about the robbery.

As we entered the over lit, rather ostentatious antique shop, named 'The Heirloom Studio', I also noticed a solid silver Art Deco fruit bowl which I had last seen in Dora's display cabinet at Hampton House.

The proprietor, his eyes too light a grey for comfort, a greasy comb-over and a shifty smile showing a row of decaying teeth, confirmed that browsing was perfectly acceptable.

Engaging Delicia in conversation, he complimented her on her American accent as his lecherous gaze slowly roamed over her body, eventually settling on her large diamond engagement ring.

On the assumption that we were wealthy American tourists with plenty of disposable income he agreed to us photographing several items, with a view to them becoming wedding presents.

"My fiancé, Lord Grensom, lives in Scotland and he will need to agree my choices," Delicia told him.

"I fully understand Madam," creepy proprietor, almost bowing, deferentially replied.

The Christopher Dresser jardinière with stand, the silver Art Deco fruit bowl and several other items were photographed. The 'other items' to act as a foil.

We then purchased the brass dinner gong for Rory.

Mr Fordice, the proprietor, on the promise that we would send him a copy, agreed to us photographing him standing before his shop front then gave us his business card. Saying, "It's been a pleasure doing business with you."

We smiled as we left.

Out of his earshot I then said, "Not such a pleasure when the police knock on his door!"

"You bet ya" was Delicia's comment.

"Penny for them?" I asked an unusually quiet Delicia on our train journey home.

"I'm pregnant, about three months, not sure exactly," was her matter of fact reply.

"Is that good or bad news?" I asked.

"Ralph and I are pleased but I know mom and pop might kick up a stink. Very old fashioned, save yourself for your wedding night and all that," she said.

"Will you tell them before the wedding?" was my next question.

"Don't know. The wedding is planned for the end of June but we might need to bring it forward. Just not sure."

At that she closed her eyes and fell asleep.

After supper that evening Delicia removed the last roll of film from her camera and put it back into its cylindrical tin. It was left, along with Mr Fordice's business card on the hall table.

"Be a good idea if Ian could take them to the cops tomorrow for developing. That way then he and Dora can identify any items belonging to them which were stolen."

I telephoned Ian who was very pleased that we had the photographs and a lead for the police.

Rory and Claudette loved the dinner gong. Bonny supervised them taking turns banging it and, as we thought, Rory enjoyed placing his face against the metal to feel the vibrations.

The following day and in honour of Delicia's visit Bonny and Claudette had made cheese scones for elevenses and we gathered round the table to enjoy the treat, telling Claudette how clever she was.

Bonny would be leaving us in three months to start her

nurse training when she would be 18 years old. The children loved her and Vera had expressed concern regarding finding a replacement mother's help.

The bleeding started after lunch with one spot, followed by a gush.

Delicia said, "I'm bleeding Bettina, I suspect I'm having a miscarriage?"

She seemed quite calm and even managed a limp smile when Dr Anna arrived.

Following a conversation and a brief examination, hospital admission was the decision Anna made, immediately making the arrangements by telephone.

The haemorrhage occurred whilst we waited for the ambulance – it was as frighteningly sudden as it was, even more alarmingly, copious.

Delicia, her lips grey and no longer smiling, her skin now clammy began to drift in and out of conciousness.

The ambulance, bell clanging, transported Delicia accompanied by Anna to the Morgan Endowment hospital, known as The Morgan to local people. I quickly gathered a few essential items together, asked Bonny to meet the boys from school, and followed in my car.

I was met by Anna in the reception area saying, "Mr Sturgis is examining Delicia now and the operating theatre is being prepared."

Mr Sturgis came out of Delicia's room, Anna introduced me as Delicia's friend. He asked for information regarding Delicia's next of kin.

I explained that her fiancé was in Helsinki and her parents were in America.

His curt response was, "Inform them immediately." Then

disappeared down a corridor, white coat flapping.

A nurse told me I could pop in to see Delicia for two minutes and that she was sleepy having had an injection in preparation for her operation.

Tears filled my friends eyes as she said, "I sure am scared Bettina, the bleeding hasn't stopped."

"You must try not to worry, Mr Sturgis is a renowned gynaecologist, you couldn't be in better hands," was my attempt at a reassuring reply.

"Look after my engagement ring please," she said, placing the ring in my hand.

"I will and I'm also going to telephone Ralph the moment I get home. Do you have a number for him?"

"Hotel Kamp," she replied, drifting into sleep.

Driving back to Iona House with Anna she told me that she and Moshe hoped to be married later in the year.

Moshe was in the process of changing his last name from Salmanowitz to Salmon which would make them feel safer as the political situation in Poland was becoming less and less tolerant. She had heard from her relatives over there that a camp/prison called Dachau had opened in Germany, supposedly for political prisoners but rumour had it that Jews, gypsies, homosexuals and the handicapped would be held there.

Many of Anna and Moshe's relatives were intellectuals in senior government positions and would be leaving their home country to seek political asylum in Great Britain.

I thanked Anna for the care she had shown Delicia and went into Iona House to telephone Ralph at Hotel Kamp, Helsinki.

Later that evening, sitting back in the reception area of

the Morgan I waited for visiting time. The unfamiliar aroma of hospital antiseptic combined with the smell of heavily waxed parquet floor filled my nostrils; giving the whole situation a surreal air – and not in a good way.

The hospital had been built in a leafy suburb of Ransington in memory of a young pilot, shot down and killed in World War One. His parents insisted that the design of the building should be that of an aeroplane and that the facilities provided for patients needed to be of the highest standard. All the staff working at the Morgan were proud to do so, always offering an excellence of care.

Having had her operation and now back in her room, room 7, Delicia lay motionless in her bed. It would have been impossible to distinguish her face from the white pillow case were it not for the mass of red, curly hair separating them.

A tall stand held a bottle of blood labelled A negative. Drip, drip it went down the rubber tubing, flowing slowly into Delicia's arm. A glass chamber about half way along the tube enabled the nurse to watch the flow of the blood.

A nurse sat beside the bedside. "Your friend is to be 'specialled.' she said.

"What does that mean?" I asked.

"It means that a nurse will be observing her around the clock until her condition is no longer considered critical," she replied.

I touched the diamond engagement ring, now on a chain around my neck and, although I do not consider myself a religious person, said a small prayer.

"When do you think she will wake up?" I asked.

"Not sure, but don't worry, it takes time to get over the

anaesthetic," the nurse replied.

"My friend's fiancé will be here as soon as he can, he's travelling from Finland," I said.

"That could take a few days. I'm sure she will be pleased to see him. She should be awake by then," the nurse said in a reassuring voice.

Drip, drip, silently dripped the blood. I could see it through the glass chamber.

Another nurse came into the room and I was asked to wait outside whilst they washed and turned Delicia.

The reception area was quiet, the visitors now gone home; the hospital settling down for the night. I found a discarded copy of The Times and attempted the crossword puzzle.

I was doing quite well, about half way through when I saw Mr Sturgis enter Delicia's room with Matron. He didn't stay long and when he came out I asked him how she was.

"Your friend will survive," he said, "But she's been through the mill and will need to convalesce. Her parents are in America, I understand."

"Yes, but her fiancé will be here as soon as he can. He is travelling from Finland."

"Finland! Oh yes I recall you telling me that, stay with her overnight if you wish.

"Thank you," I said.

The night nurse relieved the day nurse, who gave an impressive report on her patient's condition before leaving.

Another bottle of A negative blood was brought and much checking and form filling was done by two nurses prior to changing the bottles over.

I also noticed a tube draining into a glass jar hanging on the side of the bed. The nurse explained to me that Delicia had a catheter into her bladder and the liquid in the glass jar was urine. She reassured me that this was perfectly normal for a patient having had gynaecological surgery.

The lights were now lowered for the night, except for the one needed by the nurse to see her patient and to fill in her charts. I was offered and accepted a cup of cocoa and a blanket.

"Have a doze if you want," said the nurse, "I'll wake you if Miss Van der Linden stirs."

Nurses came and went throughout the night including the night Sister doing her round with a torch. Swan-like white cap fluttering above the navy blue shoulders of authority, silently covering the wards and rooms in her black rubber soled shoes.

Drip, drip – I must have fallen asleep. My dream, a muddle of antiques and missed trams and trains – nonsense, as dreams often are.

Time for another wash and turn with two nurses so I left the room to stretch my legs. Whilst standing in the shadow of the main entrance I observed nurses going for dinner at 1am in the morning. Prior to that I had never given a thought to the dining arrangements of those working the night shift.

They looked very wide awake and cheerful unlike myself who just craved sleep.

"Poorly girl in room seven," I overheard one say.

"Yeh, she's a bleeder, always the same with gingers," came the reply.

"She'll need watching like a hawk and no mistake," said first nurse.

At 5am there was a gentle knock on the door of room 7 and Ada quietly entered.

"I heard about Delicia last night," she whispered. Frank called into the farm to tell me so I hitched a lift into Ransington on the milk wagon. Left a note for Miss Dent on the way."

Surprise for a moment caused me to be momentarily speechless, but then I asked Ada how she had actually found the hospital.

"Geoff, he drives the milk wagon knew where it was. He dropped me off on his way to the dairy," Ada said.

"But you don't even know Delicia," I said.

"I know, but I know you and I'm here to hold your hand, if you know what I mean. By the heck she looks awful pale," remarked Ada.

I stayed until about 6:30am knowing that I must be home in time to take John and Alfie to school.

Going through the reception area I said, "Good morning" to a domestic cleaning lady who was waxing and polishing the floor.

"I'm giving the floor a right good bumpering today," she said. "There's a Lord coming to visit."

'New travels fast,' I thought.

I was back at the hospital by noon but there was very little change. The blood transfusion had now been replaced by a bottle of clear liquid.

"It's saline," the nurse said, observing my curiosity.

"How is she?" I asked.

"The bleeding has more or less stopped and I would say your friend is slightly improved", she answered.

The afternoon passed slowly – Delicia lay white and still in her bed.

As she did for a further night and day.

On the afternoon of day three I'd popped back to Iona House to check that the boys had everything they needed and were behaving well for Vera and Bonny.

I was back at the hospital by 6pm to find Delicia sitting up in bed, pale but no longer in receipt an infusion.

Ada had introduced herself and explained that I'd had to go home to check on the boys.

Delicia had heard that Ralph would be visiting and was visibly excited.

"Please help me do my hair. It's such a mess. I hope you've brought me a nightdress, this hospital nightie is hardly a fashion statement."

"Sure have," I replied, thinking, 'I must be picking up her colloquialisms.'

Fresh nightdress, pretty bed jacket, hair brushed and tied up, lipstick carefully applied and her diamond ring back on her finger, Delicia sat in bed with her Vogue magazine ready to receive her fiancé.

"We'll go now. Ralph should be here before too long and it's best you have time with him on your own," I said, inwardly saying thanks that my little prayer had been answered.

"Thank you Bettina and Ada. Bit of a rocky couple of days, but look at me now. Tickety Boo- as you English say."

"I'll pop back tomorrow," I said.

"Did Ian pick up the film and card from Mr Oily?" Delicia said.

"It's Mr Fordice," I said.

"I know, but don't you think Oily suits him better?" Delicia said.

"I'll find out today. You try to rest until Ralph arrives."

"Okay" she said smiling.

– 135 –

As we drove out of the hospital car park at 7pm a tall, handsome man got out of a taxi. He had tousled hair the colour of corn looked tired and was in need of a shave, I instinctively new it was Ralph walking briskly towards the main entrance.

'Now he definitely does have the look of a Lord about him', I thought, 'in spite of the fact that he had slept in his clothes on the journey, which had taken three days.'

"He looks fit," commented Ada.

"He looks tired," was my observation.

"Yey but tired in a fit kind of way," she said.

"Come to think of it I feel rather tired myself," I remarked.

"I know," she said. "I'm buggered meself."

Delicia was discharged from hospital after a further four days.

Percy drove her, with Ralph, in the Daimler to great aunt Eliza's home in Gosforth.

On strict instruction from Mr Sturgis, Delicia was to rest as much as possible and eat nourishing food, which would not be a problem. Telling her parents, with their old fashioned values, the reason for her hospital stay might, on the other hand, be a different matter.

My hope was that they would be thankful she was alive.

18

The Renovation

Flinging the windows open wide on a sunny, late May morning I felt excitement at the thought that, today, Agatha and I would be meeting the architect regarding the rebuilding and refurbishment of Providence House.

All had been agreed with the insurance company and the house, now propped up and surrounded by scaffolding, had been cleared of all its charred contents. Nothing could be salvaged.

Mr Seagrove, the architect, spread his plans over the dining room table in Iona House causing more than a frisson of excitement for Agatha and me. Such precise and beautiful plans, with words such as bathroom, boot-room and orangery in his neat architects handwriting.

One room, Agatha and I both agreed upon, was the sewing room, which had previously been the morning room.

We had had several enquiries regarding making ladies nightwear and underwear. Our plan for the future was to start a small business making exclusive silk and lace tap pants, cami-knickers and nightdresses.

"Would you like me to contact some builders on your behalf or do you have one in mind?" Mr Seagrove asked.

We agreed that it would be helpful if he obtained quotes for us.

The following day a letter arrived for us.

Willow Wood Farm.
Little Laxlet

May 25th, 1934

Dear Miss A. Dawson and Miss B. Dawson,

As you know my dad, Albert Dixon, has the tenancy of the farm and I'm writing on his behalf.
Please could we meet up with you as there are several repairs needed on the farmhouse including a re-thatch.
I know some builders who would do a good job at a good price and we would be willing to go half on the money side of things.
Yours sincerely,

Albert Dixon (son)

We met with Mr Dixon and his son at Groat Cottage. Both men dressed alike in green tweed suits and matching flat caps.

They presented their list of repairs.

"Your dad didn't do much int' way of repairs over 't years," said Mr Dixon senior.

"That's true," replied Agatha, "I agree we must make the farmhouse fit for you to live in."

"Any chance we could put a bathroom in and electric?" asked Mr Dixon junior, adding, "I've a mate who is a plumber and another one a builder and another one who's a sparky."

"I don't see why not. Get prices for the work and we can take it from there," I replied.

Young Mr Dixon, now blushing to the roots of his brillianteened hair said, "Can I ask you one more question?"

"Yes, of course," I replied.

"Do you think your friend Ada would go out with me?"

he said as he shuffled his feet uncomfortably and twisted his cap in his hands.

"I don't know, I'll certainly ask her but couldn't you just ask her yourself?" I replied.

"I've tried, but every time I go into the police station there is always someone else there," Albert said.

"Okay then, I'll ask her for you," I said, realising that young Mr Dixon must be a very shy man.

Adam was busy with his exams and I didn't want to disturb him, however I thought a Good Luck card from us all, including Pip, would be supportive.

I missed him but knew that these finals were extremely important so he needed peace and quiet to study.

In response he sent me a postcard, a view of boats on the river. The message read:

Thank you for the card.
Up to my eyes with revising.
Exams almost over.
Looking forward to meeting Pip.
Love,
Adam

Ada's response to a date with Albert Dixon was not so positive.

Rookery Farm
Little Laxlet
June 4th, 1934

Dear Bettina,

Albert Dixon – I DO NOT think so. He's stick thin with a

neck like a giraffe – not my type – AT ALL.

By the way I've finished with Bernard the butcher. I got sick of hearing about his stamps and there's a limit to how many sausages I could eat. I was fed up with him I suppose.

I'm foot loose and fancy free but definitely don't want to date Albert Dixon – no thank you.

Work is going well. Miss Dent is having an affair with Hector, the commercial traveller from Rhumen's – who by the way is married!!!!Says his wife doesn't understand him, believe that one if you like – ha, ha!!

They meet in the back office in her lunch time and spend a lot of time in the stationary cupboard. I suppose Rhumen's do supply all the stationary to the police station so they do have an excuse I suppose. She makes him little butterfly cakes but I'm not sure, yet, where they go for sex. Miss Dent lives with her sister, another Miss Dent, so that would be awkward to say the least.

I'm due an appraisal soon so I'd better keep in with her.

Love,

Ada. xxx

PS I passed Providence House the other day on Raven and men were working on the roof. One wolf whistled at me, the cheeky bugger, so I put my fingers in my mouth and gave a loud whistle back. When he looked my way I gave him the V sign and rode off.

Iona House was as busy as ever, Agatha had now fully moved into Groat Cottage, possibly to escape the noise of the children and Pip.

Mabel Scribbins had become a favourite for Rory. He followed her like a shadow and between them they developed a language of signs. Claudette was always on hand to interpret if necessary as she seemed to understand everything Rory wanted.

"Lady Mcleod," Mabel said as we sat around the kitchen table enjoying our morning snack. "Would I be allowed to play my accordion for the children? I think Rory would enjoy it."

"He would I'm sure, but Mrs Handyside might not, after all you are here to help her."

"Oh, I would play with him in my own time, I wouldn't take any time off from helping Mrs Handyside."

"It's certainly worth a try and should be fun for the children," said Vera. "When Rory is two we are going to try him with a hearing aid."

"Thank you, I'll bring my accordion tomorrow," said Mabel who I knew missed her own child who had died of diphtheria when the little girl was about the same age as Rory.

"Did you hear that Iris Mathias is married?" Vera said.

"What, after a 15 year engagement, I'm flabbergasted," I said.

"Yes," Vera continued, "she phoned the office at Landsdown Short and told the welfare secretary she was taking a week of her due holiday. On her return she wished to be known as Mrs Chapman and that she and Mr Chapman were honeymooning in Scarborough."

"Well I never," said Mrs Handyside, "his mother died in April so there was no one to stand in their way."

We all then toasted the newly weds, Mr and Mrs Chapman, with our mugs of tea.

I had a momentary vision of Iris driving Jeremiah wild with passion in her Woolworths tap pants and Evening of Paris perfume, him in his cap and socks. Moaning with ecstasy and lying in each others arms at last without interference from his mother.

A letter arrived from Delicia.

High Stones
Gosforth

June 10th, 1934.

Dear Bettina,

I am still at Great Aunt Eliza's and not feeling as well as I should be. Ralph has had to go back to Scotland on estate business, but that was following a consultation with another gynaecologist.

Mr Sturgis had told me before I left hospital that it would be unlikely that I would ever carry a pregnancy to full term. However Ralph and I wanted a second opinion. Sadly the second opinion was the same.

I had never even thought about having a child, but it is strange how I now think about it a great deal and it makes me sad.

Mom is here in Gosforth and staying with my grandmother who is Aunt Eliza Janes's best friend and lives quite near. Did you know that my mother is your great aunt's God Daughter? The wedding is going ahead but not this month – I haven't felt strong enough to be involved in it. It will now probably be at the end of September here in the Parish church.

If possible please will you be my chief bridesmaid with Ada also as a bridesmaid and I would like John and Alfie to act as pages if they are willing. Tell them they will not have to wear velvet pantaloons or anything fancy; but highland dress.

Tomorrow Mom wants me to travel to London to meet a

dress designer called Mr Norman Hartnell who will make my wedding gown. I'll send you details so that we complement each other on the big day.

Aunt Eliza Jane has shown me the family wedding veil. It is hand made Carrickmacross Irish lace and so lovely that Mr Hartnell will need to design me a gown to match the veil.

My dad is in Scotland with Ralph's family – no doubt discussing the dowry.

I always look forward to your letters so please write soon.

Love,

Delicia

xxx

PS Any news on Ian and Dora's stolen goods?

PPS Please could you send me Ada's address.

As if by telepathy Dora arrived at Iona House later that day.

"I have news," she announced, lighting a black cigarette and placing it in a holder as she came into the tower room.

"News?" I responded, opening a window.

"Yes news. We have retrieved most of our possessions, from York of all places" Dora said.

"That's good news indeed. So the photographs were of help to the police?" I said.

"Oh yes, I can't even begin to tell you how wonderful it is to be reunited with ones antiques," she said, smiling.

"I'm sure you must be delighted. Was your diamond necklace recovered?" I asked.

"Unfortunately no. The police think it will have been dismantled and sold on as loose diamonds. Such a shame, but we were insured," Dora affirmed.

"I expect Ian will buy you another one," I said.

"Yes that is the plan. However I just popped by to say how clever your friend was to take photographs. Especially of the owner which was his nemesis darling and no mistake. Please will you thank her for me," Dora said.

"Delicia is staying with great aunt Eliza Jane if you would like to write to thank her yourself," I suggested.

"That won't be necessary Bettina, I'm so incredibly busy these days but I would like you to thank her on my behalf – mustn't forget our manners now must we!" she said.

"I will," I said, whilst thinking, 'Dora wouldn't know manners if they jumped up and slapped her in the face'.

"So who's this little poppet then?" exclaimed Dora, moving over to Pip.

Pip gave a low growl, something I'd never heard her do before but it expressed exactly how I felt.

"This is Pip. Did you ever get round to having a guard dog?" I asked.

"No, no, no, no, too many hairs on my Persian rugs. We had electronic gates installed instead," Dora said, backing away from Pip.

"Electronic gates," I repeated somewhat stupefied by her inane comments.

"Anyway must fly darling. I just called as I knew you'd be thirsting to hear our news. By the way what's that racket I heard coming from the conservatory as I came in?", she added.

"Oh, that will be Mabel playing her accordion for Claudette and Rory," I replied.

"Whatever for? Terribly common. What is Vera thinking of to allow tunes which would only be heard in a public bar," was her parting shot as she ran down the stairs.

Peace at last, I thought, and what would she know of tunes played in a public bar?

19

Durham

A t the end of June I received a letter from Adam.

June20ᵗʰ, 1934

43 Sugden Street,
Durham.

Dear Bettina,

My exams are over and I'm longing to see you. Is there any chance you could come here to Durham for a weekend. Mrs Beason says we can stay with her then perhaps we could go to Denstag and I'll introduce you to my family.
I'm due to travel to Germany in two weeks with that newspaper job I mentioned so it would be great to see you before I leave.
Love,

Adam. xxxx

Vera agreed to look after John and Alfie for me and the weekend in Durham was hastily arranged for July 7ᵗʰ and 8ᵗʰ.

"Ohhh! 'e sounds lovely your Adam," Mabel said, dusting the morning room.

"Yes he is," I replied, wondering which clothes to pack for what had the promise to be a romantic weekend.

"I expects you'll marry 'im. A big weddin' like your friend's avin," Mabel said.

"I don't know about that," I replied. "We've only seen each other a few times."

"Bonny 'll be leavin' soon, goin' off to be a nurse at that big 'ospital in Newcastle," said Mabel.

"Yes, that's true and we'll all miss her," I said.

"Well I might as well come right out with it," Mabel said. "I'd like the mother's 'elp job. Do you think you could put in a good word for me with Lady McLeod? I'd be ever so grateful, really I would"

Unsure how to react to this statement I confirmed with Mabel that I would talk to Vera about the possibility.

A text book on Anatomy and Physiology was the leaving gift we jointly decided would be appropriate for Bonny.

This was presented to her by Claudette at a small tea party we held on Bonny's last day with us.

We were all sad she was leaving and wished her well with promises to keep in touch.

The following day the new mothers help, Mabel Scribbins, took up her duties looking after Claudette and Rory.

Mrs Handyside was not pleased to have lost her cleaner two days a week but Vera assured her that a replacement would be found. She then confided in me that the decision regarding Mabel and the mother's help position hopefully was the right one.

Early on the morning of July 6th I woke to hear someone vomiting in the bathroom.

Vera, looking pale, was sitting in the Lloyd Loom chair resting her face on the cold tiled wall.

"I think I'm pregnant," she said, before retching again into the basin. "Been feeling like this for days now. No energy; but don't worry you can still leave the boys with us. Angus will help. I want you to enjoy your weekend."

The following day Adam looked a little surprised, but took it well, when we met in Durham for what we had hoped would be a romantic weekend for us both.

Two boys aged 10 years and 7 years in tow did not equate to romance! Although he seemed very pleased to meet Pip for the first time,and she him.

Mrs Beason, as always, wearing her steel curlers, turban, slippers and wrap-around pinny, seemed delighted to accommodate two extra guests and said, "The put-u-up in the kitchen will suit them perfectly."

John and Alfie enjoyed boating on the river and eating ice cream in the market place.

After looking at the castle and a visit to the cathedral we had an egg and chip tea in a cafe. The shelf/lift, situated in a hatch in the wall, transported the fresh food from the upstairs kitchen down to the cafe, then the empty plates were taken up on the shelf/lift for washing.. The boys seemed to find this engineering phenomenon fascinating and even years later would offer the spectacle of plates of food on a moveable shelf as the highlight of their weekend in Durham.

"I'll watch the boys tonight if you two love birds want to go out somewhere," Mrs Beason said. dragging on a woodbine. "We'll be fine, won't we boys, I've got a set of dominoes, we can have a game."

Adam and I accepted her offer and followed her advice; the 'somewhere' being a stroll by the river, sometimes arms round each others waists, sometimes holding hands, relaxed and enjoying just being together on a warm summers evening, Pip sniffing and snuffling in the river bank.

Stopping at a pub we met some people Adam knew and

were invited to join them at their table in the garden, I was introduced to his friends, mostly men and three girls. The men seemed friendly enough but the women looked me up and down from under their severe fringes and over coloured eye lids, scrutinising my appearance from top to toe in, what I can only describe as, a disdainful manner. Not quite knowing how to react I just looked back then stared into my shandy, hugging Pip who was now sitting on my knee.

Listening to the conversation, which was mostly, discussing the political situation in Europe, with much assurance that Britain would not be drawn into the unrest. One young man spoke passionately about the strikes in Spain and how he felt sure there would be civil war there. Should that happen he was prepared to fight in the name of Spanish democracy.

The three girls seemed not to want to have a conversation with me but sat smoking, looking disinterested and examining their finger nails. Leaving me with my only option, which was to listen in.

"Mummy and Daddy will be simply livid when they discover I've fluffed my exams," said the girl named Flossie.

"I know, it's fucking annoying, I'll have to marry that creep Mungo now to keep them off my back, if I've bombed, which by the way I seriously suspect I have," said the girl named Fanny.

"Yah! Fucking annoying. Is that Mungo with the monocle?" asked Flossie.

"Yah, That's him. He's loaded. Something in the city, banking I think," said Fanny.

"I've heard he has a big dick," said the third girl who was Bunty.

"Yah! Eye wateringly huge," said Fanny.

"Have you seen it?" asked a wide eyed Flossie.

"No, gave it a good feel once and it's positively Gy-nor-mous darling, but he prefers the boys, swings both ways don't you know," said Fanny.

"Not a recipe for happiness me thinks," said Bunty

"Marriage is what you make it. Mummy told me that. Provide an heir and a spare then take a lover," said Flossie.

I was beginning to feel as bored as they looked when the third girl, Bunty, fixed her piercing cold eyes on me and asked, "And what are you reading Betty – Adam did say you are Betty, didn't he?"

"I don't go to university and my name is Bettina," I replied, which had the effect of eliciting a scornful snort from all three, whom I gathered from their conversation I could not have helped but overhear, were reading English.

My reply prompted Bunty to then again turn her back on me, returning to huddle with her friends. One of whom, I couldn't help but notice, rolled her eyes and raised her eyebrows.

I was unsure whether the behaviour of these girls was a deliberate attempt to make me feel inadequate or simply that they were bad mannered in the extreme.

Whichever it was did not matter, my heart felt like lead and I wanted to leave.

However more jugs of beer were ordered.

The debate eventually changed from Politics to Literature and Adam happened to mention that I had read Kafka's Metamorphosis and that I could also do the Times crossword.

Ignored all evening, suddenly the three 'blue stocking bitches' were galvanised into giving me their full attention.

Kafka was to be part of their studies next semester, if they had passed their exams. In which case they would be returning to university and Metamorphosis was on their reading list.

I gave a brief account to prove my knowledge of the work but declined to have any further conversation or debate with them.

"Adam, I think we need to go, I'm concerned that Mrs Beason might be finding the boys a handful," I said, desperate to leave.

I wanted to say something flippant, something to make the girls more self aware, something humorous and clever, but all I could come up with, whilst inwardly fuming, was, "Goodnight."

Aunt Eliza Jane would have said that if the three of them were put in a bag and shaken not a grain of personality would have fallen out.

Walking back to Adam's digs he said, "How did you get along with the girls?"

My reply was in the form of a question, "Did you really think I'd enjoy sitting with three of, possibly, the rudest girls in Durham. All they talked about was money and big dicks!"

"Ouch, as good as that!" was his laughing response.

I joined in with his laughter thinking that to see the humour in any situation is always a good thing.

John and Alfie had not settled to sleep on the put-u-up in Mrs Beason's kitchen.

Following a farcical episode, rather akin to musical beds, I ended up sleeping in the kitchen with Alfie whilst John went into my bed in the box room. When I woke up John was also asleep beside me, as was Pip.

So much for romance!

The following morning the four of us were singing 'One Man Went To Mow' as we motored in the Morris Minor towards Denstag, with Pip sitting between the boys on the back seat.

Mrs Rutherford met us at the gate where she hugged Adam as though she hadn't seen him for years.

Adam's dad came in from the garden with a box of fresh vegetables and said, "Hello pet, I'm glad our Adam's brought you home at last."

Then looking at me a bit closer said, "But I'm certain we've met afore."

"We might well have," I replied. "I was here with my Auntie Vera, to visit the quilters the summer before last."

"That's reet, and these two bonny lads are cracking footballers. I remember them playing in the lane. Caused quite a stir they did," he said.

"Our Jenny's coming over later, I think you met her at the quilters," said Mrs Rutherford. "She's my niece, me and her mam are sisters."

"Jenny is lovely, she really encouraged me with quilting and helped me get started on making a quilt," I said.

"That's great to hear because she's very excited to see you again," she said.

"Do you quilt Mrs Rutherford?" I asked.

"No Bettina, I used to but now I knit, mostly guernseys, jumpers and the like. Is chicken okay for dinner, do your little brothers like chicken?" she said.

"They certainly do, they eat like a couple of young horses," I replied.

Following our delicious Sunday lunch, or dinner, as the

Rutherford's called it Jenny called by and brought her latest quilt to show me; it was fabulous. It must have measured 6 feet long and 5 feet wide with appliqué work so fine and delicate the tiny stitches could hardly be seen. "I've copied the style of the old American Baltimore quilts and now I haven't a clue what to do with it," Jenny said.

"It will be an heirloom for your family but too gorgeous to use," I said, admiring the delicate baskets and circles of flowers. "I hardly dare touch it."

"Go on, have a feel, quilts are stronger than they look. It must be two years since you were last here," she said.

"I know, we didn't get over here last year because Rory was a baby and the others all had whooping cough," I said.

"How's Vera?" Jenny asked.

"Fine," I answered, not wanting to say that Vera thought she might be pregnant.

"Real surprise, her having a baby and not knowing she was expecting," Jenny said.

"I know, baby Rory took us all by surprise. He's almost two now and a very busy boy. Did you know he is deaf?" I said.

"I didn't. That's a shame, will he be going to the Deaf School?" Jenny asked.

"I don't know, but I think they said they are going to try him with a hearing aid when he has had his birthday," I answered.

We chatted on whilst various other family members called in to say hello, making me feel most welcome.

"Did you ever finish your grandmothers garden quilt?" Jenny asked.

"Yes. It's in the car," I said.

The football game was in full swing, dustbins for goal posts. John and Alfie were happily running and kicking the ball with the other boys. Adam and Pip had gone to the greenhouse with his dad.

We were looking at my quilt which I'd lifted out of the car, when Jenny asked, "Is it serious then, with you and our Adam?"

"Not sure, but I hope so," was my shy but honest response.

"I suppose you know he's going to Germany and France," Jenny said.

"Yes I do," I replied.

"We're all dead worried for him, what with all that's going on over there. Riots, strikes; as for that Hitler, he scares the living daylights out of me. Me Auntie Sybil, his mam, is worried sick. She won't show it but she is, I know it," Jenny said, obviously concerned.

"So am I, I'll be pleased when he's home," I added.

Mrs Beason and her neighbour both in steel curlers and turbans were sitting on the front doorstep having a gossip when I dropped Adam off in Durham.

We hugged and held each other tight, trying to hide behind the car and hopefully not in full view of the ladies.

Our kiss was warm and tender if brief, a kiss so special my heart turned over.

"I love you Bettina," Adam whispered in my ear.

"I love you too, please come back safe and sound," I whispered back.

"Eee yer can't beat young love," said Mrs Beason, from her vantage point on the top step."

Here have a tab Nora," she continued, taking a packet of

cigarettes out of her pinny pocket.

"I know," said the neighbour, lighting up. "Takes you back, dun it."

"He's going abroad next week," said Mrs Beason

"Ooo never in the world, abroad's full of foreigners, they eat horses and snails. I wouldn't like abroad," responded Nora, flicking ash onto the pavement.

"Smothered in garlic," said Mrs Beason.

"What is?" asked Nora.

"Everything!" Mrs Beason replied.

With his goodbye kiss still warm on my lips I drove out of Durham towards Ransington, the promise of letters with foreign stamps, news of his work in Europe.

We had not had much time alone together to discuss past, present or future.

Is it serious? Jenny had asked. My heart told me yes, as did the tears pricking behind my eyes. Pip, with her amber, almond shaped eyes gave me a look of complete understanding, licked my hand than settled in the passenger seat beside me.

"Can I have the foreign stamps?" asked John, bringing me back to reality.

"No, I WANT THE STAMPS," shouted Alfie.

"How about you share the stamps," was my solution. "Now watch out for the RAC man on his motorbike and remember to return his salute. We'll soon be home."

20

The Wood

The air was heavy with the scent of the old Bourbon rose, wafting in on a gentle breeze from just outside the kitchen window at Iona House.

The weather in August 1934 was proving to be hot in the day and not much cooler at night. Claudette was planning her third birthday party with help from Mabel; I watched them in the garden, from the kitchen window, the sun dancing on Claudette's blond, bobbing curls. Rory was having his nap which gave Mabel the opportunity to teach Claudette how to play musical bumps, the hokey-cokey and the intricacies of pass the parcel.

It had been three full weeks since Adam had travelled in an aeroplane from London to Germany. His letters told me of huge political change. Hitler had appointed himself leader of the country, giving himself the title of Fuhrer.

Restrictions on Jews regarding employment and marriage to none Jews gave Adam concern.

The newspaper reporter he was working with had begun to send his copy back to his newspaper office in England using code. Reading between the lines I quickly understood that I must be very careful regarding the content of my letters to Adam and did wonder if they ought to be coded too. However I decided to keep to domestic issues, nothing political. I told him of Delicia's impending wedding, about the children and, of course how much I was missing him.

A drawing of the design of Delicia's wedding gown by Mr
Norman Hartnell was sent to me with a letter.

High Stones,
Gosforth

August 9th, 1934.

Dear Bettina,

*The wedding date is now firmly set for September 22nd and the
invitations are being sent out this week.*
Hope you like the drawing of my dress.
*Would you have time to come to Newcastle so we can visit
Bainbridges where Aunt Eliza Jane tells me there is a good
choice of fabric for the bridesmaids dresses for you and Ada.*
I'm feeling much stronger and can't wait to see you.
*I have written to Ada who says she is delighted at the prospect
of being a bridesmaid.*
Love,

Delicia

xxxx
Ps Have you heard from Adam?

Vera's pregnancy had been confirmed and although now
feeling less nauseous she still needed to rest each afternoon.
Nurse Jean Fellows was calling each week to check her blood
pressure and ensure that she was eating a nutritious diet and
not vomiting. The new baby was due to be born in February
1935.

John and Alfie were having their six week summer break
from school so I wrote to aunt Eliza Jane and asked if we

could visit her for a week and make a holiday for the boys. I did mention Pip in my request.

She was delighted and reminded me to pack my swimming costume and swimming trunks for the boys.

On arrival we were welcomed with hugs, kisses and orange cake.

Before we were even through the front door an excited Alfie was asking, "Can we swim in the pool now?"

"Of course you can, but can you actually swim?" asked aunt Eliza Jane.

"Oh *yes*," replied Alfie with confidence.

"I'm not sure that either of you can swim safely. Rule number one is that neither of you go anywhere near the water unless there is an adult with you. We'll take it slowly, do you both understand what I'm saying," I said in what I hoped was an firm tone.

"I think Bettina needs a nice cup of tea and a piece of my cake first. Then I promise we'll go and look at the pool," said aunt Eliza Jane.

Over tea and cake Eliza Jane told me that her daughters, Gladys and Winnie, both excellent swimmers, had offered to give the boys swimming lessons each morning at 7:30 am before leaving for work at *Gibbs Funeral Care*.

Delicia, looking much better, suggested we go to look for fabric the following day as she and her mother had an appointment with Mr Norman Hartnell in London later in the week.

"I shall be carrying white flowers in my bouquet so choose whatever colour for the bridesmaids dresses you would like. Does Ada have a preference?"

"No. She said she is happy to leave it to me."

We settled on pale aqua satin with cream satin detail on the neckline. The pattern we chose was called 'The Great Gatsby Bridesmaid Dress' and was the latest fashion. The design was slim fitting with a high draped neckline at the front, dipping too a low V at the back with a bow detail. The sleeves were short and the skirt had several below the knee panels for ease of movement.

Delicia had a generous financial allowance from her father for the wedding which meant she paid for all the fabric, the pattern and a pair of above the elbow satin gloves for me and Ada. Our shoes were to be silver and Delicia asked me to purchase mine and she would reimburse me the money and to please tell Ada the same.

Delicia told me that visits to Mr Hartnell were exciting and now her mother wished to be dressed in one of his 'mother of the bride' outfits for the wedding, necessitating several trips to London.

"There is still so much to do," she said. "Mom is driving me nuts which I believe is usual at this stage."

John and Alfie had an appointment with a tailor the following day to be measured for their kilts, shirts and buckled shoes, all of which would be hired.

"Do you think Vera would agree to Claudette being a flower girl?" Delicia enquired.

"I should think so, but we will need to ask," I said.

"If she agrees could Claudette's dress be white?" Delicia asked.

"Yes. Do you want me to make it?" I asked.

"Of course. I wouldn't trust anyone else."

We were both laughing and it was good to see my friend laugh.

I had sent my Great Uncle Tobias a postcard, saying that we were in the area and would be calling on him and I hoped he liked dogs.

Arriving at Ford House I was surprised to see yet another FOR SALE sign at the entrance to the long laurel lined drive.

A young woman, whom I recognised from my last visit, answered the door and I asked her if it was okay to leave my car in the clearing outside her house.

"That will be fine," she said. "Tobias is expecting you and looking forward to meeting his great nephews and your dog."

"I'm surprised to see your house up for sale so soon after you moved in," I remarked.

"Yes, we are moving to Edinburgh with my husband's work. But to be honest this place is very remote, there are no neighbours or children near for my two to play with," she said.

"I agree, it certainly is remote here, miles from anywhere. See you before we leave," I said walking with Pip and the boys towards the wood.

Uncle Tobias was tending his bee hives when we arrived at his pretty stone cottage, the sight of which, as before, I found delightful. Looking frail in his summer suit and sun hat he did not hear us at first, then Pip gained his attention. As he looked in our direction a smile beamed on his face from ear to ear.

"Welcome, welcome my dear Bettina. Please introduce me to my great nephews."

"This is John who is 10 and this is Alfie who is 7. Boys this is your Great Uncle Tobias," I said as they all shook hands.

"Come inside, come in and Pip too. I have prepared for your visit with lemonade and cake, I hope you find lemonade and cake agreeable."

"How are you Tobias?" I asked, although I could see he had lost weight and now used a walking stick."

"All the better for seeing you. I rarely have visitors these days so today is a treat. Yes a treat."

He then addressed the boys. "Tell me about school, do you prefer the arts or science?"

"I like maths," said John. "Next year I'll be taking the exam for the grammar school."

"That is most interesting, most interesting. Did you know I used to be a teacher of maths and Latin?"

"Yes," said John. "Bettina told us. You must be very clever to be a teacher."

"And what about you Alfie, do you enjoy school, what is your favourite subject?"

"Football and cricket," Alfie replied, without hesitation.

"How wonderful, I was never good at football. Cricket was my game. Played for my school. Would you like to see the photographs?"

Tobias then took us, slowly, around the cottage looking at the framed photographs of cricket teams adorning the walls. They were mostly school photographs but then we came to a picture of Tobias with Wilfred Rhodes and Donald Bradman, all looking very happy staring out at us.

"Taken at the test match. I went every year until recently. That was my annual treat.

Would you boys like to see the bees or 'apes' in Latin John? You will learn Latin at the grammar," Tobias asked.

"Will they sting me?" asked Alfie, as he moved tentatively towards the hives.

"Not if we take care," replied Tobias, obviously enjoying himself.

Pip seemed happy to sniff around the garden for a while before joining me to lie in the shade of the garden bench, where I sat just relaxing and thinking about nothing much at all.

Tobias was teaching John and Alfie about the bees and I kept hearing Latin words such as 'regina apis', 'gerula', 'masculum apes'. Buzz, buzz, a balmy summers day, the boys learning about bees, unimagined perfection I thought, enjoying the sun dappling through the trees. The smells and sensations of the garden, drowsy bees,drunk on nectar were my thoughts as I dozed.

My Great Uncle came and sat beside me.

"The boys have gone into the wood," he said. "I told them it was permissible to climb the trees. Does that have your consent? I do hope so, I loved climbing those very trees as a boy."

"Of course, that is fine. Has Pip gone too?" I asked.

"Yes, she certainly is a bundle of energy," he replied.

We sat together for a while, quietly listening to the silence of summer, watching wisps of cloud mix with the blue of the sky.

"You say John and Alfie are your half brothers," Tobias said.

"Yes," I replied.

"Please don't think me impertinent as I know your mother died, but what of their father?" Tobias asked.

"He is Herbert Flitch, currently in prison for participating in a serious robbery from the army camp near Little Laxlet," I explained.

"Ah, yes I recall the case," Tobias said. "It was all over the papers at the time. Terrible business, terrible business. Embarrassing for the boys, but news grows old, life moves on."

"The boys are unaware of their father's imprisonment and they don't ask me any questions. Of course I would have to be truthful should they do so," I said.

"Quite so, quite so," he murmured.

Again we sat in comfortable silence for a while.

Tobias then said, "I have a proposal Bettina, please hear me out."

He then went on to tell me that as he had never needed to pay rent or mortgage nor had a family, he had accumulated sufficient savings to help with educating John and Alfie.

My protests were in vain and Tobias was insistent that trust funds for both boys would be arranged forthwith. Monies to be accessed only for educational purposes.

"The boys will not be going to a fee paying school," I said.

"That is not of consequence," he replied. "You Bettina are beautiful and I suspect you also are wise. Wise enough to know that they will require school uniforms, books, pens, etc. Oh! And of course cricket equipment." A smile lit up his face when he mentioned cricket.

I felt that thanks were inadequate but simply said, "Thank you Tobias, I really appreciate your help."

"Now," he said, changing the subject, "I have assembled a salad for us, please would you call the boys."

The dim, cool dampness was a stark contrast to the warm, sunny garden. I heard John and Alfie before I saw them up a tree on the far side of the wood.

"Careful now, come down, we are going to have some-thing to eat. Where's Pip?" I said.

We all called "Pip, Pip, Pip" as we searched the wood hoping to hear her bark in response.

She was too busy to bark for us, foraging in a mound of rotting dung which looked as though it might have originally been a dead fox.

"Phew! What a stink," said Alfie.

"Look at the maggots!" exclaimed John.

"We can't take Pip into the cottage so smelly," I said, pulling her away.

"There's a pump over there in the stable yard, said John, "We could wash her."

Pip didn't much like being sluiced in the cold water but there was no way she could have gone into the cottage or car smelling as she did.

"How did you know about the pump in the yard?" I asked as we walked back to the cottage.

"The lady in the bonnet told us about it," they said.

"Which lady in a bonnet?" I asked.

"Well, I said to John how thirsty I was and this lady said, "There's a pump over there beside the wall in the stable yard, have a drink from it," Alfie explained.

"Where did you meet this lady?" I asked.

"In the wood, she just appeared," they both agreed.

Pip bounded ahead and soon we were back in the cottage.

Tobias had prepared a delicious salad with bread, cheese and ham. All brought earlier in the day by his friends Mr and Mrs Waggerton who lived in Hexham and had a car. They called every day with his Times newspaper and provisions and took him into town, should he need to go.

Following our salad we enjoyed scones with butter and honey accompanied by a cup of tea.

"Tobias, the boys met a lady in the woods today, she wore a bonnet, do you know her?" I asked.

"That will be my mother Hannah, she often visits; in fact I don't think she ever left," he replied.

A most peculiar sensation snaked down my spine.

The boys helped me to clear the table, wash and dry the dishes whilst Tobias napped in his chair.

I wrote the names and dates of birth of John and Alfie on a sheet of paper and put it on the sideboard as I'd been asked to do.

He woke to say goodbye. I had told him that Delicia was to be married the following month and he sent her warm wishes and a gift of a jar of honey.

An evening hush was falling over the wood as we entered. I could smell moist fungus; the narrow path meant single file only, so no holding hands. Grasses and foliage brushed our legs as we walked in the fading light. Would we meet Hannah in her bonnet? Hannah who had never settled and visited often!

'Don't be silly.' I said to myself.

"Let's not dawdle, darkness is falling," I said to the boys.

I could see the picket gate, we were almost out of the wood, almost in the clearing where I'd left the car. The boys raced ahead.

Almost there, almost at the gate. My senses were heightened with, what I suppose was, apprehension. Mam would have called it 'nerves'.

Before I saw her an animal shrieked, then there she was, wearing a blue bonnet and a simple shift of a dress in grey.

She was young, beautiful and serene. Her face drifted close to mine, blurringly close. Smiling seraphically she said quietly, "Love makes you vulnerable" as she disappeared.

I felt rooted to the spot, momentarily hypnotised. The

boys were calling Bettina, Bettina.

As I walked through the gate the last remnants of sunlight warmed the car.

I knocked on the front door of Ford House to say good-bye to the owner.

"I think we may have a buyer for the house," she said.

"That's good, will it be another family?" I asked.

"No, a charity are interested in purchasing the house to turn it into a school for girls. It's a big rambling place so it should be perfect," she replied.

On our drive back to High Stones in Gosforth the boys were keen to talk about having a swim in aunt Eliza Jane's pool.

"We are really good at swimming now. Will you come in for a swim Bettina?" asked John.

"Yes I will, but I think we all need a shower first, especially you two."

"What about stinky Pip?" asked Alfie.

"I agree she needs a good bath," I said, opening the window to allow the smell of dead fox to escape.

21

The £5 Note

Early September 1934

"I know it's 'ard to believe but it's true!" exclaimed Mrs Scribbins to Mrs Handyside as they sat enjoying a morning cuppa at the kitchen table at Iona House.

"Bit by a jelly fish I 'erd," she added. "Giv 'im blood poisoning."

I'd walked in on a conversation, referring to Jeremiah Chapman, which I knew to be true, although the jelly fish was purely anecdotal. Vera had told me that, indeed, Jeremiah Chapman was dead and his widow Iris had taken one weeks compassionate leave from the typing pool at Landsdown Short to make funeral arrangements.

"They've only been married a few months," said Mrs Handyside. "Paddling in the sea he was, down at the coast so I heard."

"Just goes to show. Hi don't think 'e ever wanted to be a married man, makes you think don't it?" commented Mrs Scribbins with a sigh.

"The funeral is next Monday. Another biscuit Mrs Scribbins. Shall we go?" asked Mrs Handyside.

"Yes. Mind you she'll get the 'ouse and the car. Don't mind if I do," Mrs Scribbins replied, taking another biscuit.

The front door bell rang.

I opened the door to Iris Chapman (nee Mathias) dressed

in a black coat, hat, gloves, shoes and bag with a lilac silk scarf just peeping out at her neckline.

"Come in Iris. I'm so sorry to hear about Jeremiah. How can I help?" I said, steering her away from the kitchen and into the morning room.

"Well, it's really Percy I've called to see. Someone told me he is an excellent driver and a patient driving instructor," Iris explained.

"He is, but he is our chauffeur not really a driving instructor."

"I have a car now which is just standing there doing nothing, so I'm going to learn to drive it, I might as well," said Iris.

"I think Percy might be in the garage, shall we go and see?" I said, escorting her through the garden to discuss driving lessons with Percy. Wondering if he would enjoy the 'Evening in Paris' perfume wafting from behind Iris's ears.

"That was Iris Mathias, I mean Chapman. Wants Percy to teach her to drive," I explained to Mrs Handyside and Mrs Scribbins, as I went back into the kitchen and my cup of tea.

"Learn to drive his car and him not even buried!" exclaimed Mrs Handyside.

"She's not letting the grass grow under 'er feet – and oo can blame 'er! Replied Mrs Scribbins.

Ada and I were roughly similar in size, although she was taller.

My plan was to cut the bridesmaids' dresses out and stitch them to first fitting stage.

I would then visit Groat Cottage, as would Ada, then we could try the dresses on and make any adjustments.

The partially made dresses were packed neatly in a box and with Pip beside me I drove to Little Laxlet on a beautiful early Autumn day.

My mood was happy, having received a letter from Adam to say he was now in France, had been to an art exhibition and hoped to be home in time for Delicia's wedding.

The boys were now old enough to walk back to Iona House from school together and Mabel had offered to make them their tea; so I was not in a rush which, for me, made a change.

Parking the car on the green I went over to look at Providence House which now had a new roof and windows.

The garden was trampled and flattened but because the weather had been fair the builders had made good progress. Agatha had told me she was happy enough living in Groat Cottage but hoped to move back into Providence House before Christmas.

A small fire glowed in the grate at Groat Cottage, which was welcoming.

"I have a book with pictures of kitchen cupboards for us to look at. The builders left it," Agatha said.

"It's so exciting Agatha," I said, "choosing a kitchen, getting just what we want. The very latest designs."

"Do you like green and cream?" Agatha asked.

"I do; and how would you feel if we have an Aga, a cream one?" I asked.

"They do look nice but how would I get on cooking with it?" she said.

"You'll be fine once you grow accustomed to it," I assured her.

We looked at the pictures and made our choice of units, sink,taps and Aga.

Agatha also opted to have an electric cooker in the scullery, to use until she was familiar with the Aga.

"Frank is thinking of moving in to Providence House with me if that's all right with you," Agatha said.

"That's fine. A good idea, you don't want to be rattling around in such a big house on your own."

"I've bought a car, an Austin seven. Frank can drive and having a car makes life much easier for me," she said.

"I agree, I don't know how I'd manage without mine," I replied, adding, "We shall need new furniture."

"I know," Agatha said, laughing. More shopping!"

Then added in a more serious tone, "Do you think you will ever move back to the village?"

"It would be difficult, much as I'd like to. You see John is taking his exam for the grammar school soon and I really don't want to disturb his education at the moment," I replied.

"I understand," Agatha said, "but you will come and see us sometimes and don't forget we have promised ourselves a shot at running our underwear business."

"So we have. That can be our project for next year," I said.

Ada arrived at Groat Cottage, rather hot and sweaty, having ridden her bike the two miles from Burside. "Miss Dent said I could have an hour off to attend to an emergency," Ada said, breathlessly.

"What emergency?" I stupidly asked.

"I'll think of one on my ride back," was her reply.

Ada tried on her dress and I pinned the few necessary minor adjustments.

My dress also required a few tweaks and Agatha did the pinning.

"Frank and I have had an invitation to the wedding," Agatha said, "I'm not sure why, we don't know the bride or the groom."

"No, but you know my great aunt Eliza Jane," I said.

"It's going to be a VERY posh do," said Ada expressively, "I can't believe I'm going to be a bridesmaid."

"I know it is," said Agatha. "Frank and I will be shopping next week for our new outfits."

"The reception is in a castle in Northumberland," I added, feeling the excitement mounting.

"What! a real castle? Really old and history an' all that," exclaimed Ada.

"Yes. The owner is a friend of the Marquis, who is Ralph's father," I added.

"Bloody hell," said Ada. "It'll be like Hollywood, I'll be shitting me-self with nerves on the day."

"You'll be fine," I said, whilst thinking – 'perhaps a few tips on etiquette might not go amiss; or perhaps my friend might add a frisson of interest to what might otherwise be a rather stuffy crowd with her idiosyncratic use of language'!

A few days later Mabel was helping me to measure Claudette for her 'wedding dress' as she called it.

The dress would be made from white crepe fabric, a simple style with a sash made from the aqua satin of the bridesmaids' dresses. We would all be wearing a circlet of fresh flowers in our hair.

I noticed that Mabel was red eyed and appeared to have been crying.

"Is something wrong?" I asked.

"I don't have anything smart to wear," answered Mabel, whilst gently persuading Claudette to stand still.

"I know I won't be a proper guest, just looking after Claudette and Rory but I want to look nice," she added.

She looked so sad but I just knew I didn't have the time to make another garment before the wedding.

Then I heard myself say, "Leave it with me, I'll see what I can do."

She visibly brightened up.

'I must be mad', I thought

I was helping Mrs Handyside change the children's beds when she said, "It's getting serious with Phyllis and my Stanley, could be an engagement before too long."

"That's really wonderful news," I said. "They make a perfect couple, you must be pleased."

"She's growing on me I have to say," said Mrs Handyside, smoothing the bottom sheet.

"If they are happy together that's all that matters," I said, plumping up a pillow and thinking about Mabel.

"Something on your mind Bettina?" she asked.

"Well, yes there is," I hesitantly replied.

"I knew it, I can read you like a book. What's the problem?" she asked.

I explained about Mabel's situation and how not having a decent coat to wear for the wedding was upsetting her.

"Shame your not the same size, you could lend her yours," Mrs Handyside said, shaking out a sheet.

"I don't think I have a coat dressy enough for a wedding," I said.

"You might not, but I know someone who has, and she is the same size," she said, smoothing down the top cover.

"Do you, who?" I naively asked.

"Dora. She'll have loads of coats. Wardrobes packed to the gunnels. Bound to have a smart coat and Mabel is a very similar build to Dora," said Mrs Handyside.

"What's this about Dora?" asked Vera who had joined us in the bedroom.

Mrs Handyside then explained to Vera that Mabel had a problem and to borrow a coat from Dora would solve it.

They then both looked directly at me.

"Oh no, no, no, no. I'm *not* asking Dora!" I almost shrieked.

"Well I'm not," the both proclaimed in unison.

"You'll be perfect," Vera said, in a persuasive voice. "Think of all the favours you've done for her in the past and it would only be a loan.

Later that evening, having written myself a script, I telephoned Dora and asked if she might have an outfit that Mabel could borrow to wear for the wedding.

"Mabel, Mabel who?" she said, in a scratchy tone.

"Mabel Scribbins, our mothers help. She is about your build," I said.

"Surely she is not a guest at the wedding," Dora said in a shocked voice.

"No, but she will be looking after Claudette and Rory and, of course, wants to look smart for the occasion," I said hoping she would understand.

"Can't this Mabel girl just go out and buy something?" was Dora's response.

"Mabel doesn't have any money to do that," I replied hoping to tap into her softer side.

"I don't know if I have time to look through my things, I'm incredibly busy and I need to shop for my own outfit for the wedding. I'll be choosing mine from Fiskers of course, all their clothes are designer only," she said.

She didn't seem to be softening.

"I was sure you'd have a nice coat tucked away in your wardrobe, perhaps one you don't wear any more," was my final attempt.

"No Bettina, I'm frightfully sorry but it has to be no. Goodnight," she said firmly, putting down her phone which ended the call...

My thoughts towards Dora, as I replaced the telephone receiver onto its cradle, were vaguely menacing. I felt disappointment rise in my throat – my attempt had been futile.

The following morning a plain brown envelope, with my name handwritten on it, appeared on the kitchen table, much to the interest of Mrs Handyside and Mrs Scribbins.

"On the back mat when I came in this morning," said Mrs Handyside, pointing to it.

"Might be from a secret admirer," said Mrs Scribbins.

I picked up the envelope. I had their full attention.

Inside was a white £5 note and a short hand written note which said

For Mabel to buy a coat.

I explained that my attempt to persuade Dora to lend Mabel a coat had been unsuccessful but now that did not matter as I would give her the £5 from a well wisher.

"That Dora, heartless, completely heartless, that's what she is," said Mrs Handyside, pouring the tea.

"She's going away to Switzerland after the wedding," I said. "Seeing a doctor over there about that cough she's had for ages. The air is so pure it should do her health good."

"Health indeed, you can believe that if you like," said Mrs Handyside, adding "Health, humph, more likely she'll be going for those monkey gland injections."

"Switzerland, I 'eard it's lovely there. She'll be dying 'er muffy 'air afore she goes," said Mrs Scribbins.

"Dying what!" I exclaimed.

"'er muffy 'air. She likes to look matching in the nuddy, if you knows what I mean," she repeated. "My neighbour, Esther, cleans up at 'ampton 'ouse 'nd she told me. Dora dyes 'er muffy 'air"

"That's it then. I bet you a pound to a penny she's going for them monkey gland injections," said Mrs Handyside, sipping her tea.

"Oooo! I've 'eard of them. Hagony in yer arse but does wonders for your face, she'll come back looking ten years younger," said Mrs Scribbins.

By this time we were all laughing with tears running down our faces.

I'd never heard of monkey gland injections but thought to myself, 'Who needs to go to the music hall with these two for company!'

22

The Cricket Pavilion

It was **unseasonably** warm for late September. The bride would be leaving for the church in a grey Rolls Royce Phantom, from great aunt Eliza Jane's house. Telegrams had been arriving since 7am, wishing the happy couple well. Then the telegram boy brought one for me.

Was stuck on the French coast.Stop Now on a train in England. Stop Love, Adam Stop

Momentarily my heart sank, Adam would not be here in time for the wedding.

I sat on the bed surveying the room, I saw two aqua satin bridesmaids dresses and the page boys outfits for John and Alfie; so no time to dwell or feel miserable as I had a job to do.

As chief bridesmaid I was required to look after the bride and keep her calm in readiness for the ceremony.

Ada, on her best behaviour, opened the front door to the florist and accepted delivery of the bouquets, headdresses and button holes. Fragrance from the flowers permeated up the stairs, uplifting and changing my mood, helping me to deal with the day ahead.

I dressed John and Alfie in their kilts, shirts, jackets and buckled shoes. Brushed their hair and ensured they had straight-as-a-die side partings.

"You both look the most handsome pages ever," I said to them. "Now please don't touch anything other than that chess set."

Ada and I changed into our bridesmaids dresses and put our circlets of fresh flowers in our hair.

"My don't we scrub up well," I said.

"Bloody gorgeous, more like," Ada added.

The dresses had turned out well and I knew we would not let Delicia down.

Delicia, looking more beautiful than I've ever seen her, wore her Norman Hartnell bridal gown with style. The fine white silk fabric, embroidered with sprigs of heather, clung to her figure as though she had been poured into it. The long train, embroidered with Ralph's family crest, pooled delicately beside her.

The previous evening I had attached the antique family veil, made from Carrickmacross lace, to the exquisite diamond tiara which was the 'something borrowed'. Lent to the bride by her future mother-in-law, Alexandra, the Marchioness of Mear, who had worn it at the coronation of King George V.

I placed the tiara firmly on Delicia's red, sometimes unruly curly hair, Ada and I took a gasp of breath and both commented on how beautiful she looked.

"All brides look lovely on their wedding day," Delicia said modestly, "but thank you."

I arranged the veil around her face thinking she looked almost ethereal, certainly awe inspiringly majestic, ready to meet her groom.

Mr Nick Van der Linden entered High Stones to be greeted by great aunt Eliza Jane, wearing her dazzling new outfit in pale grey silk and matching toque hat with an impressive ostrich feather. Her nine rows of pearls filled her neckline and diamond and pearl ear-rings hung from her ears.

I looked down into the hall from the landing to see the father of the bride standing tall and erect in his tailcoat wedding outfit, placing his top hat on the hall stand table.

"Good morning Eliza Jane," he said, as she fastened a sprig of white heather in his buttonhole.

His whole manner and demeanour spoke of wealth and hard business. 'Not a man to get on the wrong side of,' I thought.

Aunt Eliza Jane then addressed Nicholas Van der Linden as though he were a small boy, "I shall be leaving for the church within the next few minutes with Gladys, Winnie and their husbands, followed by the pages and bridesmaids. Escort your daughter with pride in your heart Nicholas, she is a very special young woman."

Listening to the peal of bells, we waited by the big, oak front door of the church for Delicia and her father. A photographer clicked away as they emerged from the grey Rolls Royce Phantom.

The organ began to play Handel's 'Jesu Joy of Mans' Desiring'.

With Delicia on her father's arm we began to process slowly up the aisle towards the alter, where Ralph and his older brother Quentin, Vicount Frume, the best man, waited.

John walked immediately behind the bride and her father, supporting the bridal train.

Then Alfie and Claudette, holding hands.

Ada and I followed the children, feeling pleased that all had gone well so far and the bridal party looked stunning.

The sun shone through to rose window, dappling shades of colour onto the affluent guests.

Mrs Van der Linden, looking beautiful in her pink Norman Hartnell ensemble, sobbed quietly into her lace handkerchief, as mothers of the bride frequently do.

During the ceremony I had the opportunity to look more closely at the bridal veil noticing many bees, butterflies and dragon flies embroidered around the edge.

Keeping one eye on John, Alfie and Claudette and listening to the service I attempted to count the bees but quickly lost track.

Ralph, looking ruggedly handsome in his kilt, vowed to love, honour and keep her. Delicia then returned the vow – until death us do part.

Total joy eluded me at this perfect of perfect weddings, marred by the fact that Adam was not there.

Although no longer in France, where was he? On a train in England – that's all I knew. My mind was wandering so I quickly re-focussed.

As the bridal party exited the vestry following the signing of the register, the organ boomed out 'The Arrival of the Queen of Sheba'. We now processed down the aisle towards the door.

Eight soldiers in highland dress who were from Ralph's old regiment, assembled as guard of honour outside the church. Kilted, swashbuckling, good looking young men, they made an archway of swords for the bride and groom to walk under whilst a piper piped the tune 'Mairi's Wedding'.

Confetti thrown, photographs taken. We all then climbed into limousines to be transported to the castle.

Ada was quiet other than commenting. "I've changed my

mind, moved the goal posts."

"Meaning what?" I asked.

"I'll definitely be marrying money," she replied.

I had to admit that the guests attending the wedding had an unquestionable aura of money about them and, judging by the outfits and perfume the women were wearing, were good at spending it.

Ralph's older brother Quentin, heir to the title Marquis of Mear and best man at the wedding was unmarried. His girlfriend Arjana Zabala, a tall, stunningly beautiful black woman, wore a long purple and pink dress which caused a sensation as it was in the traditional African style including a huge, colourful matching head-wrap.

Quentin's speech was witty and entertaining, mentioning some of Ralph's misdemeanour's as a young boy, as well as the time they served together in the army. He complimented the bridesmaids, pages and the flower girl.

The bride and groom were then toasted in the finest champagne, and the wedding cake was cut by Delicia and Ralph using a full regimental sword.

Following the meal and speeches Vera and Angus came over to say goodbye. They were leaving early to take a tired Claudette and Rory home but I thought Vera looked upset.

"Something wrong?" I asked her.

"See that cheeky woman over there, the one in the red hat," she said. "Well you'll never believe what she just said to me."

"No. What did she say?" I replied.

"She said, taking a chance going to a wedding with a baby due any minute, could have had it in the church," Vera explained.

"What a cheek," I said, "You're not due for ages yet."

"Another four and a half months."

"Now don't let her upset you. Some people just don't think before they speak," I said, whilst thinking, what a cheeky insensitive cow the woman in the red hat was.

The band began to play and Delicia and Ralph performed their 'first dance'. Mr Van der Linden escorted Lady Alexandra Mear on to the dance floor then the Marquis invited Mrs Cynthia Van der Linden to dance. Very traditional and lovely but having the effect of making me feel even more lonely for Adam.

Not so Ada who, having enjoyed several glasses of champagne, was dancing with an extremely handsome, bearded young man in a kilt whom I recognised from the guard of honour.

Ian and Dora were seated not far away from me so I wandered over to say hello.

"Lovely wedding, are you having a good time?" I asked.

Looking as though she had swallowed a wasp, Dora said, whilst putting down her champagne glass, "Your little match girl looked rather well turned out for someone with no money."

Ian looked uncomfortable and rubbed the side of his nose which I took to be a signal not to disclose the fact that Mabel had received £5 from a well wisher.

I smiled in what I hoped was a serene manner and replied to Dora, "I assume you are referring to Mabel, she did didn't she, quite lovely in her new coat. I think the russet colour suits her well."

"She must have had a win on the horses or worse, that coat looked expensive to me, she must have found the money from somewhere. A walk down at the docks perhaps!" was Dora's vitriolic response.

I knew exactly what Dora was insinuating and had, until now, thought she couldn't sink any lower with her unkind remarks and bitchiness.

Feeling my anger grow I simply said, "Enjoy your holiday in Switzerland" as I walked away.

"I will darling, I will," she said, holding her pearl cigarette holder up to her lips then inhaling deeply.

Later and out of earshot of Dora, Ian apologised, telling me that she was unwell and possibly the reason she was in such ill humour.

"I didn't realise she was so poorly," I said.

"Yes Bettina. It's her lungs, she is flying to Switzerland in hope of a cure. May need an op."

"Are you going with her?"

"No, determined to go it alone, tough as old boots," he replied.

"I hope all goes well. Please let me know how she is," I said, "And thank you for the £5."

"Mum's the word," he said.

"Mum's the word," I added, going back to my table.

John and Alfie were enjoying playing hide and seek with some of the other children at the wedding.

When they came to the table for a drink of lemonade I asked them, "Have you seen Ada, I haven't seen her for a while?"

"No," replied John.

"She's playing hide and seek," said Alfie.

"What, with you children?" I asked.

"Noooo silly. With a man," Alfie said.

"Which man?" I asked.

"The man who gave out the leaflets in the church," said Alfie.

Two of Ralph's cousins had been ushers so I imagined it must be one of them.

"What makes you think they are playing hide and seek?" I asked Alfie.

"Because …" said Alfie, before taking a gulp of his drink, "…because they are hiding under that table over there, over there next to the wall. The one with the big white cloth to the ground."

Not quite believing my ears I asked "Did you actually see them under the table?"

"Oh yes. The leaflet man was lying on top of her, I think they must have been having some sort of a cuddle. He told me to buzz off as it was their hiding place."

"This castle is great for hide and seek," John added as they both ran off with their new friends.

I looked across at the table wondering if I should go and look but before I could a kilted gentleman asked me to dance.

The band played 'Have You Ever Been Lonely'. 'Apt', I thought.

The dance was slow, my partner had two left feet but at least I wasn't sitting moping any more.

"Lovely wedding," I said.

"Aye, grand," he replied.

"Have you known Ralph long? I asked, hoping to develop the conversation.

"Aye, army," he said.

"Excuse me," a voice behind me addressed the young soldier who immediately stood aside.

I couldn't believe it. Adam swept me into his arms. The band played 'If You Were the Only Girl in The World.' and suddenly I felt as though I was dancing on a cloud. I'd convinced myself that he wouldn't make it and now he was here; pure joy bubbled up inside me.

To be dancing together was wonderful. He held me close, our eyes gazing into each others. It was so good to see him, I simply immersed myself in the moment.

Winnie and Gladys agreed to look after John and Alfie whilst Adam and I went for a walk in the grounds of the castle.

We had a great amount of catching up to do, so many questions, so many answers.

"You look beautiful Bettina, I've missed you so much," Adam said, slipping his jacket around my shoulders.

"I've missed you too. I thought you wouldn't make it today," I said.

"Transport problems like you wouldn't believe. Missed the first ferry, some sort of work to rule in France," he explained.

"Never mind, you're here now," I said.

With a gentle finger he traced my jaw.

My finger ran slowly round the rim of his ear, then over his dark eye brows.

He gently squeezed my arms before encircling me in his. I held his face in my hands and with our eyes wide open our lips met in a soft delicate kiss.

We inhaled each others breath, I felt the warmth of his skin, the kiss became firmer, passionate, a timeless moment, heat rising, each wanting the other.

Feeling the need for privacy we followed the path which

led to a building which was not locked. We went in.

Judging by the equipment stored there, illuminated only by moonlight, it appeared to be a cricket pavilion.

Closing the door we immediately indulged in a deeper kiss, a kiss which quickly heightened into a sensuous, passionate kiss. Adam's hands caressing my back and my thighs. My arms encircling his neck.

A half moan, half scream rent the air.

We froze.

Then a further moan, quieter, but a definite moan.

"Stotter Diddies, ooooh, Stotter Diddies," an excited and somewhat breathless male voice said.

Adam and I stopped kissing and were now looking at a curtain from behind which the noise had come.

"Stotter Diddies, Stotter Diddies, They're amazin, you're amazin", said the Scottish male voice.

"Yes … oh yes. Ooo lovely … just there," moaned a female voice which I recognised as Ada's.

I then noticed the aqua satin bridesmaid dress draped over a folded chair next to a kilt.

"You're driving me crazy, just fuck me, fuck me. Never mind me tits," Ada demanded.

"I'm gantin fur it the nuw, fare gantin!" he was shouting as we crept out of the cricket pavilion.

Needless to say our moment of passion had passed. We just looked at each other in the moonlight and burst out laughing.

"Stotter Diddies, what do you suppose that means?" Adam asked.

"I havn't a clue, but it sure excited the Scotsman," I replied.

Back on the dance floor Adam held me close, our steps in unison; I couldn't take my eyes off him.

However, in my peripheral vision I noticed that Ada had returned with her soldier partner. They smooched as they danced, his hand stroking her aqua satin clad buttocks, his eyes fixed on her cleavage.

I caught her eye. She winked and gave me the thumbs up sign which her partner did not notice. I thought, 'There's no doubt about it, Ada now knows what's under that Scotsman's kilt.'

***

Translation from Doric which is a dialect in North East Scotland:-
Stotter Diddies – beautiful breasts.
Gantin fur it the nuw – wanting it very badly now.

23

Jude

Late October 1934 and the nights were drawing in. A good fire crackled in the grate and we would be having toasted crumpets with melting butter and honey for tea. I had spent the afternoon hand quilting my latest quilt, with Pip snoozing beside me, the time had passed quickly and now I waited for John and Alfie to return home from school. Today they would be later than usual as both had been playing football for the school team. It was now nearing 5pm, chilly as the day became dusk, just before darkness fell.

The boys now cycled to and from school and had strict instructions to put their bikes away in the garage and not leave them in the back lane.

A postcard from Rhodesia, for each of them had arrived that morning from Delicia and Ralph where they were honeymooning. The pictures of the wild animals were wonderful and the stamps would be perfect for the boys' albums.

John and Alfie burst into the warm kitchen, socks down to their ankles, dirty knees, shirts hanging out of their trousers, one tie askew one missing and the filthiest of hands.

"Have you put your bikes in the garage?" I asked, followed by, "Wash your hands please, we're having crumpets for tea."

"Yes we have and there's a baby crying in the back lane," John said.

"A baby, whose baby?" was my response.

"Just a baby, we didn't see it, just heard it." Alfie replied.

"Are you sure it was a baby and not a cat?" I asked.

"No it wasn't a cat, it was definitely a baby," John said with conviction.

"It's almost dark now. I can't imagine there'd be a baby out there at this time. Now wash your hands again, and properly this time," I said.

I started to put food on the table but the thought that a child might be crying in the back lane stuck in my mind.

"Okay then we'd better go and have a look just to be sure. I have a torch, show me where you think this baby is," I said as we all left the house.

Pip found the baby first, it was no longer crying.

Wrapped in a white damask table cloth an abandoned baby was tucked away behind a dustbin near the garage.

I picked the child up, hoping it was still alive I held it close to my chest wrapping my cardigan around it; the bundle in my arms felt very damp and cold.

Vera was in the kitchen when we returned with the child, swaddled in a table cloth, which I placed on the table.

Claudette and Rory climbed up to look and were immediately interested as we all gathered around the poor, cold baby.

"It was in the lane, the boys heard it cry," I offered as an explanation.

"Is it alive?" Vera asked, anxiously.

We removed the cold, damp tablecloth. The child was breathing but not moving. His face was pink but his feet were blue. The umbilical cord was long, soft and fresh. Someone had tied a piece of twine around it.

"It's a boy!" John and Alfie exclaimed in unison.

"What shall we call him?" asked John.

"Humph, another boy," said Claudette, sounding disappointed.

I wrapped him in a blanket and gently held his tiny cold feet, trying to coax warmth into them.

Dr. Moshe Salmon was telephoned and, within half an hour, he brought Cow and Gate formula milk and a fresh rubber teat. Whilst we waited a glass feeding bottle had been sterilised by Vera in a pan of boiling water.

The baby woke and cried then drank the formula milk from the bottle.

Moshe explained that, as the child had been abandoned, which was a criminal offence he, as the doctor, would be required by law, to notify the police.

I, as the person who found the baby, would be interviewed by the police the following day.

In his estimation the child was only a few hours old when found and its mother may be in need of medical attention.

Alpine Lodge Orphanage would become home for the foundling and Moshe said he would take him there straight away.

We dressed the baby in a nappy and clothes which Rory had had as a newborn and wrapped him back in his blanket.

Feeling emotional, I handed the child to Moshe.

Vera said, "Would you like to go with him? I can look after the children."

"Yes." I heard myself say. Thinking, 'the baby will be lonely without me'. "Please help auntie Vera with the tea John, I won't be long."

All the children said goodbye and Alfie gave him a precious teddy, which surprised me.

I held the sleeping baby close as we travelled to Alpine Lodge Orphanage in the Doctor's car. The journey seemed very short.

With swift economical movements Matron placed the baby in a cot asking, "Does he have a name?"

"Jude, he's called Jude."

"Jude what?"

"Just Jude. I found him in the lane. Doctor Salmon thinks he was born today. Here is his teddy."

"Newborn," she said. "His mother might come forward, but like as not she won't. They rarely do."

I chose to walk home in the melancholy darkness. Warm tears rolled down my cheeks, dripping off my chin. My crumpled handkerchief sodden. I felt something no words had yet been invented to describe.

Adam was busy working at *Gibbs Funeral Care* in Newcastle and partnering ladies at the hotel tea dances. He was staying with great aunt Eliza Jane in Gosforth and we had not seen each other since the wedding.

The morning after leaving Jude at the orphanage a letter arrived for me from Adam.

High Stones
Gosforth
26th October,1934.

My darling Bettina,

I have taken a couple of days off and will be coming to see you next Wednesday, shall we go dancing or would you prefer the pictures?

By the way I have just heard this morning that I've won an exchange scholarship to study law at Harvard University so

lots to talk about.
See you on Wednesday.
Love you,
Adam.
xxxxx

"Where's Harvard University?" I asked Angus over break-fast that morning.

"America, but not sure where in America," was his reply.

The policeman called to interview me about finding the baby, taking a statement which I signed. He took away the tablecloth and said I would hear in due course.

That afternoon Pip and I went for our customary walk but not the usual route. We found ourselves at The Alpine Lodge Orphanage.

Pip was not allowed into the nursery but one of the house -mothers agreed to watch her for me.

"I've come to see Jude," I said.

"Jude? We haven't got a Jude," answered the nurse in charge.

My heart sank, had his mother claimed him? If so then I should be happy.

I tried again. "Jude, I brought him in last evening, he was a foundling."

"Oh! The foundling. That'll be Martin. Matron names the foundlings and she's called him Martin. Don't think she can have liked the name Jude. He's over there, you can feed him if you like, I'm run off me feet," she said.

Pip and I visited Alpine Lodge orphanage each afternoon for the next few days, taking John and Alfie with us on Saturday and Sunday. Matron had a Scottish terrier called Logan who had a bed in the corridor outside the nursery and took no offence at Pip sharing it.

I heard the motor bike from the house before I saw it. It was Adam's latest purchase and as he rode up the drive I thought he looked more handsome than ever, even though he was wearing goggles.

Taking off his safety helmet his dark brown wavy hair sprang all over the place framing his stunningly good looking face, my heart turned over.

I ran out of the front door and into his outstretched arms. Our lips met in a firm, passionate kiss, arms locked round each other, Pip dancing and barking in welcome and for his attention.

"I have so much to tell you," Adam said.

"Me too and I have someone I would like you to meet," I said.

"I'm intrigued, who?" asked Adam.

"We'll have a walk with Pip later then I'll take you to meet him. By the way Vera says you are welcome to stay with us for as long as you like."

Adam was excited about his scholarship in America, me not so much.

"But a year, maybe more is a very long time. I'm going to miss you. It'll be awful," I complained.

"I know, I know, I'll miss you too but a year or two will soon go over. Just think Bettina, with my degree then this extra law qualification I'll stand the chance of a better job. It'll mean a brighter future for us," he said.

I liked the thought that he considered me as part of his future.

Jude was now a week old and a very contented baby. I had fed and changed him each day and spent a great deal of time just looking at the curve of his cheek, the brown silky fluff which covered his head, the way he pursed his lips and stretched his whole body when out of his nappy.

"This is Jude," I said to a rather stunned Adam. "We found him in the back lane. The boys heard him crying and there he was, cold and wrapped in a table cloth."

A friendly nurse with a round face and squidgy hands said, "There's a couple showing an interest in adopting Martin. When they arrive would you mind waiting in the corridor?"

"Martin?" asked a confused Adam.

"Matron calls him Martin, I named him Jude."

The prospective new parents arrived to view the baby, we adjourned to the corridor which had a viewing window into the nursery.

The man was fashionably debonair, black hair slicked back with Brylcreem, a snappy pin striped navy blue suit, a red tie and black and white shoes.

She was, in stark contrast, a beige woman; beige face, beige hair, beige hat, beige coat, beige shoes and handbag. The only colour she carried were her finger nails, long, manicured, carefully painted bright red with the half moons showing.

Adam and I waited with Pip and Logan in the corridor, watching the prospective parents through the internal window.

My thumping heart sinking to my boots.

The woman touched the cot without enthusiasm.

Matron picked up the baby, handing him to the Brylcreemed man, who held the child with an air of disdain.

Somewhere in a distant corridor a grandfather clock chimed 3pm.

With a mirthless smile the man handed the child back to Matron who placed him back in the cot. The woman shook her head. I read her lips which said, "No, it has to be a girl."

My heart soared. My beautiful Jude had been spared. I breathed again.

"Your beautiful Jude," Adam said as we walked back home.

"Oh Adam I would love him to have wonderful parents and a secure home, but that couple were awful," was my rather judgemental response.

"Are you sure about that. You seem to be getting very attached to young Jude."

"I'm sure," I replied, in what I hoped was a convincing voice.

"Well tonight my darling Bettina, tonight is for us. I will dance you off your feet. Take your mind off the baby, whom I'm absolutely certain will have new parents soon who will dote on him and give him everything."

As we walked Pip found interesting places to sniff and I couldn't help thinking how uncomplicated her life was.

Arriving back at Iona House Ian's car was in the drive and Percy, wearing his chauffeurs uniform, was loading suitcases into the boot of the Bentley. Unusual I thought at this time of day.

Vera met us in the hall with the sombre news that Dora had died in Switzerland.

"Dora dead! That's unbelievable … *how*?" I asked.

"Some procedure to do with her lungs, that's all we know at the moment," Vera said. "Ian is devastated as you can imagine. He's in the study now with Angus. They will both be travelling within the hour to break the sad news to Edwin and Seth. It will be a long drive, their school is in Scotland, Percy will chauffeur them."

Needless to say Adam and I did not go dancing that night.

24

The Present

Saturday morning and one week since Adam had gone America. He had boarded a French cargo ship, the 'Belle Vivienne', on the quayside at Newcastle-upon-Tyne and worked his passage as a deck hand; this being the most economical mode of transport across the Atlantic ocean. He told me in his letters that he had never worked so hard in his life but the food was good.

I now possessed a globe of the world and we, the boys and I, enjoyed finding far away places where people we knew were, or had been

"When are you going to open your present from Adam?" Alfie asked.

"Not sure," I answered, thinking I'll just become emotional as I really, really had not wanted him to go.

"Go on, you might as well. We've opened ours," John said.

Adam had given them a football each as a leaving gift.

My parcel felt heavy, very heavy for its size.

As the brown paper and string fell away a delightful bronze of a young woman was revealed. I unfurled the note which was wrapped around her; it read:-

My darling Bettina,

This is a gift for you. I found her in Paris at the art exhibition

*I told you about. She is by the sculptor Ferdinand Preiss and
she reminds me of you. Both beautiful and strong.*
*I love you in a way which is beyond my comprehension to define
and will miss you every minute of every day.*
*I will send you my address when I have it and hope you will
write.*

All my love,

Adam.

xxxx

"She's very pretty," said John, "but I'd rather have a football. Can we go to the park?"

"I'm going to see Jude," I replied, "do you want to come?"

"No way," said Alfie, "not when we've got a football match."

Pip and I walked together, swishing through the fallen leaves to Alpine Lodge orphanage.

"I think it's the birthmark on his forehead what's putting people off," said the nurse with the tight perm. "'E's a bonny lad otherwise."

The red bobbly mark, which had not been there when I found him, seemed larger and more raised now.

"I've seen 'em afore, them strawberry marks. Nevus singular, nevi plural, or haemangeoma to be perfectly correct and I have to get it right if Matron is 'ere. Like as not it'll disappear afore he's three," the nurse said.

Jude's wide deep blue eyes gazed at me as I fed him.

"Shame you can't adopt 'im," the nurse continued. "'e'll be getting to know you now, seen as you feed 'im near enough every day."

"I know, but that would be impossible. I'm single and anyway our house is full of children and another two on the way in the New Year. My aunt is expecting twins."

It had been confirmed that Vera was carrying twins.

"Ever thought about fostering 'im? Just 'till the right couple comes along, couple as wants a lad. Might only be for a few weeks?" the nurse suggested.

Vera and Angus agreed, the paper work was minimal and within a few days Jude became part of our family at Iona House. On a temporary basis – I kept reminding myself.

A letter with a Hexham postmark arrived for me.

Clay and Overton – Solicitors
Steep Lane
Hexham

November 11th, 1934

Telephone Hexham 6973

Dear Miss Dawson,

I would be grateful if you would arrange a meeting here at your earliest convenience.
There are matters I need to discuss with you which may be to your benefit.
Yours faithfully,
Nathaniel Overton.

I arranged the appointment for Monday 19th November, 1934.

It was Friday 16th November and my birthday.

The previous day Agatha had telephone me from the telephone box on the green at Little Laxlet to say that the work on Providence House was now completed, the house was ready to move into and did I want to see it.

Jude, well wrapped up and in his carri-cot on the back seat of my little Morris car and with Pip beside me we drove to Little Laxlet, arriving at Groat Cottage in time for lunch.

The baby was so well received by Agatha she could hardly bear to put him down. Hilda called in and exclaimed how handsome he was but it was a shame John and Alfie weren't with me.

"They are both doing really well at school," I said, "I don't like them to miss even one day."

Hilda seemed pleased to hear that, she'd always loved the boys.

Providence House looked wonderful. Agatha showed me around with pride.

The green and cream kitchen with the Aga taking pride of place. The new electric cooker in the scullery for Agatha to use until she became used to the Aga.

The beautiful glazed extension, now known as the orangery.

A large bathroom with hot and cold running water, basin, bath and flush toilet. Yellow and black half tiled walls.

Four large bedrooms.

Sitting room, Dining room, Boot room with flush toilet, handbasin with hot and cold running water and the Sewing room.

"What a brilliant job, a huge success," I said.

"We can decorate next summer when the plaster is fully dried out, but we can move in for Christmas," said Agatha, excitedly.

"It's a big house," said Hilda. "You'll need plenty of furniture, and then some, to fill it."

"I know, I know," Agatha squeaked. "Frank and I are going shopping ASAP."

The brass door knocker sounded three loud bangs which echoed through the empty house.

It was Ada, squealing with delight when I opened the door, hugging me and wishing me happy birthday all at the same time.

"I've tied Raven to the railings, hope that's okay. Saw your car. The baby's gorgeous. How's Adam. Heard about Dora," she babbled.

We were all in agreement that Providence House now looked splendid and the well trampled garden would recover in time.

There were then two more loud bangs on the door knocker. Albert Dixon the younger stood on the doorstep.

"Saw your car Miss Bettina. Sorry to disturb you. Hope it's all right to call," he said shyly.

"Of course it is Albert. Come in. Agatha is here," I replied. Our voices echoed around the newly plastered hall with its tiled floor.

"Well, me mates are wondering if you are pleased with the work on this house and do you want to look at the farm house, it's finished an all," he said without taking a breath and, as usual, twisting his cap in his hands. Then blushing when Ada joined us.

Agatha and I both assured Albert that we were extremely pleased with the work and yes, we would love to look at the newly refurbished farm house.

We then all followed him down the village to the farm which was only a short walk away. I carried Jude and Pip walked by my side.

Willow Wood farm house looked splendid as we approached with the wintry sun shining on the new thatch.

"Tha can turn Raven out inta t paddock if tha likes," Albert said to Ada.

"Okay," she replied, "Don't start the tour without me you lot."

The interior of the farm house was splendid.

"New kitchen, electricity and running water," said Albert, giving a demonstration by switching the lights on and off and then running the tap.

Old Mr Dixon grunted from behind his paper.

"Not one for company me dad," said Albert.

Ada walked in and old Mr Dixon's face lit up. "How do Ada love, how ist tha? Havn't seen thee in a long while."

"Very well thank you," replied Ada. "How's yoursel?"

"Ist tha still winning prizes on Raven?" Mr Dixon asked.

"I am that Mr Dixon, he's in your paddock right now," replied Ada.

"In that case I'll just go and look im ower. One of our best foals Raven, a right bonny foal and a grand horse now be all accounts," he said, slowly pulling himself out of his chair.

The bathroom extension was proudly shown off to us by Albert. We all went *ooooohh* but not in a good way. I think 'lack of a woman's touch' would be the best way to describe the stark, functional room.

"Needs some nice curtains and towels and maybe a bath mat," said Ada, echoing my thoughts exactly.

Old Mr Dixon returned and insisted on showing us the long living room, "Now with electric light," he proudly stated whilst switching the bare centre light bulb on and off several times, which seemed to delight him.

"Could do with a shade, that light, and maybe a lamp or two," commented Ada.

Agatha and Hilda exchanged, what could only be called, 'a knowing look'.

Back at Groat Cottage I changed and fed Jude. I told, Agatha, Hilda and Ada about the solicitor's letter.

"I'm a bit concerned about the appointment," I said, "but I expect it will just be to do with the trust fund Tobias had arranged for John and Alfie's education."

I went on to explain that he had been a teacher and had set up a trust fund for the boys to help if they needed anything for their education. John will be taking the exam for the grammar school soon and Tobias was very interested, even taught the boys a little bit of Latin.

"I'll come with you if you like," said Ada, "I'll throw a sickie."

"We'll look after Jude," said Hilda and Agatha together.

Mabel had already agreed to give John and Alfie their tea and Percy had already agreed to walk Pip, so now all the arrangements were made.

"It's an early start Ada," I said. "I hope 8am is not too early for you. The appointment is for 10am."

"Yep, that's fine," she replied. "I reckon it'll be about an hour in the car, maybe a bit more, so that'll give me time to tell you all about me love life."

That should be an interesting hour and a half, I thought. My love life, at the moment, I could relay in less than two minutes.

25

The Bees

It was a dull morning, with a definite chilly November wind blowing in Hexham, as we walked from the car to find Clay and Overton – Solicitors.

Ada and I sat in the waiting room with an elderly couple. The only sound being that of the gas fire which popped from time to time.

They looked rather shabby, the elderly couple, down at heel might be a good description. However I noticed that he wore expensive highly polished shoes and her handbag was made from genuine crocodile.

No one spoke, the ticking of the clock took over the room. I began to find the pattern on the linoleum fascinating and even noticed a small cigarette burn in the hearth rug in front of the popping gas fire.

"Mr Overton will see you now," said the receptionist, smiling and smoothing her skirt.

All four of us followed her into the solicitor's office where we were invited to sit down.

Silver haired Mr Overton sat behind a huge desk, piled high with files, folders, a large polished wooden box and an urn.

"Good morning, good morning Mr and Mrs Waggerton, Miss Dawson and …" he said looking over his glasses at Ada.

"This is my friend Miss Smith," I said.

"Good morning Miss Smith," said Mr Overton in a formal tone befitting the occasion, which I now realised, from a comment the receptionist had made, was a reading of Tobias's will.

We sat in silence.

Mr Overton began to read the last will and testament of Tobias Fisher.

"To my friends Mr Charles Waggerton and Mrs Virginia Waggerton I leave £200 in appreciation of the care they have both shown me.

To John Flitch and Alfred Flitch, my great nephews, I leave a fund in trust with Mr Clay and Mr Overton to be used for educational purposes.

To the the charity. 'Education For Children Without Means' I leave Ford Cottage and land, to be used as part of the school now known as Ford House School.

To my great niece, Miss Bettina Dawson, I leave the total contents of Ford Cottage and the bees with their hives. I ask that she scatters my remains in the garden of Ford Cottage.

Any monies remaining following payments to my debtors I leave to Miss Bettina Dawson."

"Does anyone have any questions?" asked Mr Overton.

Mr and Mrs Waggerton said, "No." Their scowling faces shooting me a vindictive stare, as they walked out of the office.

"Well Miss Dawson, here are the keys to Ford Cottage. The charity would be appreciative if you could clear it before Christmas and your uncle asked me to give you this box personally. It has been in our care for some time – in the safe, you understand," Mr Overton said, handing me the large, polished wooden box.

Words stuck in my throat at the generosity of Tobias.

"Thank you," I said, "I didn't even know he had died."

"I wasn't aware of that. Mr and Mrs Waggerton made all the arrangements for the cremation at the new crematorium in Newcastle.

Please contact me regarding anything to do with your brothers' trust fund when ever you need to," he said as we shook hands.

We were about to leave the room when Mr Overton said, "Oh and don't forget this" handing me the urn.

Weak shards of winter sun shone as we walked into the chilly fresh air.

"Well, those two didn't look well pleased," Ada commented.

"That's true. Perhaps they thought they'd inherit Ford Cottage," I added.

"Looked like they'd swallowed a shilling and shat a sixpence. I wouldn't trust them as far as I could spit," Ada added in her own eloquent style.

"My sentiments exactly," I agreed. "Come on I know a good tea shop. Let's have a hot drink and a sandwich."

Following lunch Ada and I motored to Ford House. Workmen were busy with the renovations and I explained to Ada that this was the house the charity now owned. Tobias had left his cottage to the same charity which would also become part of the school.

"Hello," said a smiling workman, with a pencil behind his ear. "You're the second lot of visitors today. Strange is that, we don't usually see anybody."

After explaining who we were and why we were visiting I asked, "Who else has been?"

"It was an old couple. Went to the cottage, said they had a

key. When they came back she was carrying a massive plant. Said they had to rush off but would be back in the morning with a van."

"What a fucking cheek!" Ada expostulated. "Pardon me French."

"Did you say you are a joiner?" I asked.

"Yes, a chippy, that's me, time served. I'm Neville by the way."

"Can you change locks Neville, and board up windows? I'll pay you," I asked.

"Certainly can," he replied.

"The position is this. The cottage now belongs to the charity you are working for, the same as this house. The contents of the cottage and the bee hives belong to me. If you need confirmation of this please contact Mr Overton, solicitor in Hexham," I explained, feeling anger grow in my throat at the cheek of the Waggertons.

"Right me bonny lass, now don't mither yourself. Me and Jackie here, we'll get on to it right away. The locks 'll be changed this afternoon and we'll board up all the windows. Are you stopping long?"

"No, not long. Just until about 3:30pm. If they come back please will you call the police."

"Ay we will an all. Cheeky, thievin buggers. We've got electric and the phone now in the big house so no problem."

"Thank you Neville," I said.

Carrying the urn and Ada the box I showed her the gate and we followed the path through the wood.

Ford cottage looked as beautiful as ever, even on such a chilly winters day. The bees were quiet which I supposed to be normal as it was cold.

Unlocking the door and entering the cottage was a memorable moment for me. Touching the beautiful antique furniture, which I couldn't quite believe was actually mine. However I did notice that the big azalea was no longer on the hall table.

"This is bloody gorgeous," Ada said, "did you say he lived here all by himself?"

"With his mother, Hannah, but then by himself after she died," I replied.

"Are you going to look in the box?" she asked, adding "please, please say yes, I'm dying to see what's in it."

Tied to the box were several small books and a sealed envelope containing a letter and a key. The tiny key turned effortlessly, the box unlocked. On lifting the lid there was a further box made of fine leather, lined with pale blue velvet. It contained a large ruby and diamond broach/pendant cushioned on the velvet. There were other pieces of jewellery in the larger box and another key.

The letter which had been tied to the box read:-

My dear Bettina,

The very fact that you are reading this letter means that I have now passed on.

I have never been a sentimental man but thought you should have this broach/pendant as it did once belong to your grandmother Letticia Ann.

Hannah 'borrowed it' and somehow, returning it was forgotten. I hope you enjoy the furniture, anything which is not of use to you please dispose of as you wish.

It was wonderful for me to discover you and your brothers.
With love,
Tobias.

Ps. Please do not stand any nonsense from Mr and Mrs Wag-
gerton. They have been good to me in many ways but I am also
aware that they have misappropriated money which I had en-
trusted them with.

"It can't be a real ruby," exclaimed Ada, "it's that big, as big as a pigeon's egg!"

"I suspect it probably is, as are the diamonds around it," I responded, bolting the door and moving towards the stairs.

The first bedroom was plain and tidy. A brass bed with a patchwork quilt. An oak wardrobe with a suitcase on top. A tallboy and a bedside chair.

The second bedroom also had a brass bed with a quilt. A wardrobe, dressing table and a bedside chair. There was a large wooden chest standing in one corner, it was locked.

The extra key, which had been in the polished wooden box, fitted and turned. We lifted the lid of the chest and there, wrapped in tissue paper was a skirt with a bustle and separate matching bodice. Totally fabulous, pale pink silk with tiny buttons covered in the same silk fabric. A delicate bridal bonnet emerged next, making this the perfect ensemble for a Victorian bride. Delicate undergarments, a nightdress and negligee and even a pair of silk slippers. This I realised was Hannah's wedding outfit and trousseau and it was all hand made and beautiful. There were other items, including a quilt, in the chest but we did not have time that afternoon to go through them all. However I removed the suitcase from the top of the wardrobe in the other bedroom and placed the pink silk skirt and bodice in it. I'd noticed they were heavy and wondered if there were items stitched into the hem and seams.

"Who's Hannah?" Ada asked.

A knock on the door disturbed us. It was Neville, the joiner, with the new locks

"Hannah was Tobias's mother. It's a long story, I'll put you in the picture on the way home."

I investigated the pantry and noticed at least 30 jars of honey.

Ada flirted with the Neville and his mate whilst I went into the garden to investigate the bee hives. The bees were still quiet which I supposed was to be expected in November.

I sat on the garden bench and thought back to the day Rossa-lee, the gypsy, had told me to listen to the bees. She had also told of a swaddled babby and had said, in her native Romany tongue, some pretty strong things to Dora.

Another workman arrived and they began boarding up Ford Cottage.

Ada joined me on the bench.

"What are you thinking?" she asked as we sat there looking out over the fields at the expanse of horizon and the grey, winter sky above.

"Funnily enough I was thinking about Dora and how strange things turn out sometimes," was my reply.

"I reckon that Ian is a good catch. What is he now, about forty, should be in his prime. A judge as well," Ada said.

"No. Ian was devoted to Dora. I can't see him looking elsewhere, not for a long time," I said.

"He will. I'd put money on it. He's very attractive and he looks stunning in his kilt," she said.

"How's work?" I asked, changing the subject.

"Boring, I'm not really cut out for filing. The gossip's good though. That Miss Dent and her fancy man, the commercial traveller, have taken up bridge – so they say. Just an excuse to go away for the weekend for a shag if you ask me. Emrys has gone to Manchester, some sort of detectives course and Bryn is courting a girl from Whitby which is rather inconvenient I would have thought."

"You certainly keep your finger on the gossip pulse," I said.

"Did you know Stan and Phyllis have split up?" Ada said.

"No, not Stan and Phyllis," was my shocked response. "That I find very hard to believe. How do you know?"

"It's true. Mary, on the switchboard, and Phyllis are related somehow. Their mothers' are cousins I think. Well Mary told me. Apparently Phyllis says Stan is not ready to make a commitment, whatever that means, so she copped off with his best friend," Ada said.

"That's such a shame, I thought they were made for each other," I said.

Within an hour the cottage was boarded up and the locks changed. Neville handed me the new keys in exchange for £5 – no questions asked.

The cottage was now secure.

"Thanks Miss," said Neville. "I'll notify the police if those two ne'er-do-wells show up again."

I decided to take Hannah's wedding dress with me, along with the polished wooden box, which Neville had told us was made of mahogany and valuable; also the small books which were Hannah's diaries.

"One last job before we leave," I said.

"What's that?" Ada asked.

I'm going to scatter Tobias's ashes near his bees, I think he would like that.

The wind had dropped. I ran his ashes through my fingers and watched as they mingled with the earth. I thought I heard a faint murmur of a buzz from the hives but perhaps it was my imagination.

Then I rejoined her on the bench.

"Come on then, time to go," I said to Ada, who didn't move.

"That Mr and Mrs Thingameboddy are in for one hell of a shock when they turn up with a van in the morning," she said.

"I know, what a good thing Neville tipped us off," I said.

"It's very nice sitting here all peaceful like but have you given a thought to how you're going to move the furniture, where the hell you're going to put it, let alone moving the bees?" Ada asked.

"Yes, yes and *yes!*" was my answer.

"Explain then, please, Miss Clever-clogs," she said.

"Stan," I said.

"Stan's history, isn't he?" Ada asked.

"Not quite. Remember I'm still his secretary come office manager."

"So," Ada said.

"Now Stan and Phyllis have finished he might be at a loose end and willing to do me a favour," I said.

"Jammy bugger, Bettina Dawson. If you fell in shite you'd come up smelling of roses!" Ada said.

We were laughing now.

"Mind, did you see the way that Neville was looking at me? Very sexy eyes and his bum looked cute in those dungarees," she said.

"That's as may be, but we'd better make tracks. Agatha and Hilda might be fed up with looking after Jude now and it's coming on to rain," I said.

I took Hannah's wedding outfit back to Iona House. Stitched into the hem and seams I discovered twenty gold sovereigns, a pair of fabulous ruby and diamond earrings and a diamond ring.

Had she stolen these things, borrowed them and forgotten to return them – or had Tobias Pym given them to her legitimately? I doubted I would ever know.

A week later Stan took a mate and his van to Ford Cottage and I followed in my car. We moved the furniture and everything else, including the honey, to Providence House.

Stan had another mate who worked as a rat catcher at the council who, when required, removed wasp nests and swarming bees from properties. For a nominal fee he agreed to move the hives with bees to Little Laxlet. Albert Dixon and his dad had agreed to house them in a field which bordered onto heath land.

The letters I received from Adam told of lectures, meetings with professors, other learned folk and how huge America was.

My letters to him, I felt, were much more interesting. So much had happened since he'd left and I loved telling him about home.

Jude slept in his cot beside my bed every night.

His strawberry mark now covered his left eyebrow, but to me he was perfect.

The day he gave me his first smile I fell in love with him all over again.

26

Love

It was 8:30am, a Tuesday in early December 1934, when I opened a letter from Delicia. The contents of which necessitated me to sit down.

High Stones,
Gosforth.

9ᵗʰ December, 1934.

My Dear Bettina,

We are home from Rhodesia and staying with great aunt Eliza Jane.

Our honeymoon was everything one would expect and more besides. I took loads of photographs and managed to write three articles for my friend in New York, remember, the one who edits a magazine. She says her readers go crazy for anything about the colonies.

I loved receiving your letters and hearing about the family and baby Jude. Also that Adam is now at Harvard which is my father's old university.

However I must come straight to the point. I, or should I say we; that is Ralph and I are asking you if you would think it appropriate for us to adopt Jude. As you know I will never have a child in the normal way.

When you wrote to tell us about him and his unfortunate start in life, after much discussion, we decided we would like him to be our son.

Ralph is returning to Scotland in a few days to deal with the business of the estate which has been somewhat neglected whilst we have been away for over two months.

If you agree to our proposal we could be with you tomorrow. I'm unsure how the legal side of things work but the moment you say yes, if you do say yes, we will contact Ralph's family solicitor to set the wheels in motion.

Due to the short time Ralph will be here in England please could you telephone me here at aunt Eliza Jane's to tell me of your decision.

With love,

Delicia.

xxxxxx

I felt an emotion I was unable to name, pleased and happy for Jude, but a sadness knowing he would leave me. In my heart I knew that this was an opportunity for him to have a good life with parents who would adore him.

"What's to be done?" I asked Pip, who gazed back at me with her amber eyes then licked my hand. "A hollow question," I said to her whilst, somewhat reticently, walking towards the hall to make the telephone call to Delicia, which I knew I had to make.

Shuddering in the freezing North East wind I waved goodbye to the green Riley Nine Lynx. Ralph was driving and Delicia cradled Jude, well wrapped up, in her arms.

'My baby', which is how I felt about him, was being transported, in luxury, to live a life of splendour in a Scottish castle.

Their family solicitor had quickly and efficiently made the necessary legal arrangements. Jude would be, in the eyes of the law, their son in a matter of only a few weeks.

Try as I might to hold back the tears I eventually succumbed.

With what felt like an empty heart Pip and I went back into Iona House. I gave myself a good talking to and kept repeating to myself, 'it is for the best' which I knew to be true. However, that did not make parting with a child I'd grown to love any easier. As a comfort to myself I went to my bedroom and Hannah's chest.

Kneeling beside it I unlocked it and opened the lid and lifted out the amazingly beautiful quilt she had made. I stroked it, savouring its softness and the vibrancy of the colours even after so many years. The wedding outfit, all hand stitched, tiny covered buttons, exquisite embroidery; so perfect and never worn.

Her love never properly returned or respected.

My hand then found a sepia photograph amongst the contents of the chest. It was of a woman in a bonnet, the once beautiful face now hard and worn.

I recognised her.

It was the woman in the wood and I remembered her words:

"Love makes you vulnerable."

How true I thought. For those who have never loved will

never feel emotional pain. At that moment I was feeling the pain of losing Jude; a loss I was not bearing well. A pain which ground into my heart.

"Please don't cry Bettina," a child's voice said.

Through my tears I saw Claudette standing beside me. She must have heard me crying.

"You're sad because Jude has gone with his new Mummy and Daddy aren't you?" she said, putting her arm around my neck and placing her plump cheek next to mine.

"I am," I replied.

"I understand," she said in the imperious tone of a three-year-old going on 23! A tone which belied her tender years. "Now Bettina," she continued, "Rory and I have made a shop with Mabel in the conservatory. We sell black bullets, chocolate and fish. You are welcome to step inside and buy some."

"That would be very nice," I said, standing up and taking her hand. "What kind of fish do you sell?"

"Mackerel, and I weigh it *and* I take the money," Claudette said firmly.

"Well what does Rory do?" I asked, hugging her.

"Rory sweeps the floor and stacks the shelves."

"That doesn't seem fair," I responded.

"Oh but it is. *He* is the youngest," she said.

"So he is."

Claudette continued her soliloquy as we descended the stairs. "But when the twins are born then they will be younger than him. That means he can take the money and they will sweep the floor."

"I think they might be too small to play shops for a while," I said.

"I know that," she said dismissively, "but they will one day.

Love, I thought, has many guises. Today it is in the form of a 3-year-old inviting me to play shops and buy pretend mackerel.

27

Christmas 1934

Try as I might, total joy at the thought of Christmas, eluded me. Vera was marooned in her room for most of the day reading or listening to the wireless.

"Look at me, look at me," she complained with frustration. "I'm like a beached whale."

Nurse Jean Fellows called every day now to take Vera's blood pressure and had expressed concern about her puffy ankles.

"Puffy ankles," Vera said. "Puffy ankles, I haven't seen my feet for weeks so wouldn't know. This is *sooo boring!*"

Jean, the epitome of patience, encouraged Vera to keep her legs elevated whenever possible and rest.

However, it had been decided, for the sake of the children we would try to keep the festivities as normal as possible.

A Christmas tree, fully decorated now stood in the hall. I had made, for the first time ever, mince pies for the carol singers.

On Christmas Eve morning Mabel came in early to look after the children so that Angus and I could go to Ransington market to collect the turkey and ham.

As usual, Mr Smith was doing a roaring trade, with Ada by his side serving the long queue.

"I suppose you two will want a natter in the van as per usual," he said, winking at Angus. "I've no idea what they talk about but they always have a good laugh."

"Well, they say laughter is good for the soul," Angus responded.

"How is Lady McLeod, Ada tells me it's twins?" asked Mr Smith.

"Yes. To be honest with you Mr Smith my wife is rather fed up with being pregnant, I think the whole household will be pleased when the twins arrive."

"When is she due?" asked Mr Smith.

"Another month or so to go."

"Not an easy time, not easy. Especially at this time of year. Please give her my good wishes. Will you be wanting two chickens again?" asked Mr Smith.

"Yes and thank you. I will give her your best wishes," Angus said then went off into the fruit market.

Ada and I took our mugs of hot tea into her dad's van. I'd brought some of my mince pies in a tin.

"Here's a mince pie, I made them, tell me what you think," I said, offering her the tin.

"Bit tough, but okay," she said, to my relief.

I told her all I could about Adam,which wasn't much as his letters from America continued to tell me about his law course and the university.

"Well I'm courting, serious like," she announced.

"Courting. Who? How serious?" I responded.

"I am courting Albert Dixon and we'll be getting married at Easter next year."

"Ada Smith, are you sure about this? It's not five minutes since you refused to go out with him on account of his long neck," I said in astonishment.

"Well I've changed me mind. We'll be engaged next week,"

she said.

"Has he actually proposed?" I asked, wondering if this was a fantasy.

"Not yet, but he will. I've pointed out the ring to him, in Deveraux's window. Two diamonds, illusion set, on a twist," she said, reaching for another pie.

Ada then answered a question which I had not actually asked.

"No. I'm saving myself."

"Saving yourself, do you mean what I think you mean. You and Albert are not having sex," I said.

"Correct, got it in one. I am going to be a virgin on my wedding night," she said.

'Bit late for that', I thought whilst saying, "Will that be easy to achieve?"

"Oh yes, we do that heavy petting," she said, biting into another pie. "Bertie, that's what I call him now, is bloody good at it as well. Comes from tickling trout he says."

"Tickling trout," I squeaked with incredulity.

"Oh yes. When his hand is in me draws and he starts his dandling I'm transported," Ada said, in a matter-of-fact tone.

"Transported" my parrot like repetition was starting to make me feel foolish.

"Yes, transported to paradise," she said, sighing then repeating, "transported to paradise" almost as an affirmation.

"Oh," was all I could think of to say.

"In other words, Bettina, I have one of them organisms and it's bloody lovely. Mind it makes me shout a bit," she went on.

"Where do you do your courting?" I asked, hoping it was private.

"Here and there but mostly in the long living room at Willow Wood farm. We lock the door and go for it. By the way there's a nice shade on that centre light now."

"What about Albert's dad?" I asked.

"Deaf as a post, he doesn't hear me scream," she replied.

"Scream?" I repeated in astonishment.

"Yes, scream, but purely for pleasure," she said.

"Doesn't Albert find this rather frustrating?" I tentatively enquired.

"No not at all. He likes to keep me happy and when I've had me organism I give him a wank. He loves it," she said, miming how she pleasured Bertie then reaching for the last mince pie.

I think I heard my jaw thud as it dropped open.

"You sound very compatible," I said.

"We are and what's more we're dancing at the Plaza in Ransington on New Years Eve. I'll pop in and show you the ring," Ada confidently said.

"That will be lovely," I said.

"You know your trouble, if you don't mind me saying so," Ada said, "you need a bloody good shag. That'd put a smile on that face of yours."

"Really!" I exclaimed, before we both burst out laughing.

Angus knocked on the van roof.

"Merry Christmas" we said together as we hugged each other goodbye.

Back at Iona House Dr Moshe had been called in by Nurse Jean Fellows, concerned about Vera's blood pressure.

"I would be happier if you were in hospital Vera," he said.

"Not on Christmas Eve, surely," she protested.

"I'm afraid so. Your blood pressure is rather out of control, your legs and hands are really swollen. It will be the safest place for both you and the babies. I'll telephone for an ambulance if I may and then contact the Morgan.

Angus accompanied Vera who, as she was being carried out of the house on a stretcher, instructed the driver in no uncertain terms, not to sound the bell.

"Don't worry," I'd said to them as they left. "I'll look after things and Mabel is coming in extra to help."

The Handysides and Mrs Scribbins called for their chickens and I told them of Vera's admission to hospital over a cup of tea.

"Av you ever cooked a turkey afore, or an 'am?" Mrs Scribbins asked.

"Me, no," I answered, realisation setting in that Christmas dinner now depended on me. Ian and his boys would be here tomorrow and I doubted I could cope.

"I'll come in an give yer an 'and. Do the veg if you like," Mrs Scribbins offered.

"Would you Mrs Scribbins, that would be wonderful."

"Think no more about it. Me and Mabel will be here first thing. I'll cook our chicken tonight."

"Oh I forgot your Christmas drink, please help yourselves," I said.

We all sat with our tot of brandy around the kitchen table.

"It's all off between my Stan and Phyllis," Mrs Handyside confided.

"That's a real shame," I said, "I thought they were the perfect couple."

"What will be will be," she said. "We'd best be off now, let us know if there's any news about Vera."

Angus telephoned to say that Mr Sturgis wanted Vera to

stay in hospital until the twins were born. She would probably be sedated; with rest it was hoped that her blood pressure would normalise.

The Christmas dinner was a triumph thanks to Mabel and Mrs Scribbins.

We decided to eat around the kitchen table which would be less formal with Vera being in hospital and where Angus would be spending the day.

Ian acted as host, carving the turkey with expertise, helped by myself and Mabel who waited on the guests. Dinner for ten, included Mrs Scribbins, Mabel, Ian, Seth, Edwin, the children and myself.

Seth and Edwin helped me wash and dry the dishes. I felt very sorry for them, their first Christmas without their mother and they were only 13 and 11 years old. They did not mention Dora at all.

Mrs Scribbins seemed happy to put her feet up on the kitchen sofa with a glass of port after her busy day cooking.

Later when I was putting the children to bed I reflected on how kind people were, Mrs Scribbins doing the cooking, Mabel looking after the children.

Ian had taken them home in his car which would be a rare sight in their part of town. I hoped Mrs Scribbins neighbour, Esther, would be peeping from behind her nets to witness her friends alighting from a Daimler.

28

New Year's Eve

On **December 29th,** 1934 I received a letter from Adam.

Cambridge
Boston, USA
20th December, 1934.

My Darling Bettina,

I hope you are having a lovely Christmas and not missing Jude too much.

I am now lodging with a very friendly Scandinavian family who celebrated Christmas earlier this month, rather differently to us in England.

I've booked a slot with the telephone company for New Year's Eve. As yet I'm unsure what time.

Looking forward to talking to you then, but it will only be for 3 minutes.

Love you,

Adam

xxxx

Ps I've been in correspondence with Nicholas Van der Linden, following a conversation I had with him at the wedding. He has invited me to spend time with him at one of his companies in New York. Date, as yet, to be arranged.

31st December 1934

7pm

I'd planned for a quiet New Year's Eve but now I had the call from Adam in America to look forward to, giving me a feeling of indescribable excitement; I lit the fire in the big hall so I could be near the main telephone.

Claudette and Rory were in bed and asleep, John and Alfie were happily playing chess so I settled down in the big arm chair by the fire with my quilting.

The boys had asked if they could stay up until midnight to see in the New Year. I had agreed, telling them that this year it would be quiet, just the three of us and Pip in the hall.

Around 8pm the telephone rang, my heart skipped a beat thinking it might be Adam. It was Angus.

"It's Vera," he said. "Her blood pressure is out of control again and Mr Sturgis is about to perform a caesarean section. They are preparing Vera for the operating theatre now. I thought you would like to know."

Due to my concern I was, unusually, at a loss for words, so I calmly said, "Please give Vera our love. Claudette and Rory are asleep and it's all quiet here."

"I think Ian is coming to the hospital to keep me company," Angus continued. "Can he drop Seth and Edwin off with you?"

"Of course he can. Keep in touch," I replied.

"It looks as though the twins will be born tonight," I told John and Alfie. "Ian is going to the hospital and Seth and Edwin are coming here."

"Good," they said, returning to their chess.

Within fifteen minutes Seth and Edwin arrived with their chess board and pieces.

At 8:30pm there was a knock at the door. I answered it to find Stan, looking rather lost, standing there on the door step.

"Come in and sit by the fire," I invited.

"I expect you've heard about Phyllis and me," he offered.

"I have and I think it's a real shame, you are perfect for each other," I said.

"We were, but I think she got bored with me," he pathetically stated.

"Now Stan, we have been friends for a long time so may I speak frankly?" I asked.

"You can but I doubt it will do any good," he replied.

"Phyllis needs a commitment from you. If you love her then go and tell her. Offer her something worthwhile so that your relationship can move forward," I proffered, hoping this was good advice.

"Are you sure?" he said.

"Absolutely. I think she's going dancing at the Plaza with her friend Mary tonight. Go and find her. Faint heart never won fair lady, so they say," I advised.

"Okay. If you're sure, then I will. Wish me luck," he said as he left.

At 10:30pm the telephone rang again, causing a thrill of excitement to stir within me thinking it might be Adam. It was Angus to tell me that the babies had been safely delivered.

"What are they, boys or girls?" I asked.

"Two boys and one girl," he replied.

"What *triplets!*" I exclaimed. "That's wonderful." Thinking, 'no wonder Vera was so huge.'

"How is Vera?" I asked.

"Sleeping off the anaesthetic. The nurses are taking good care of her."

"The babies, how are they?" I asked.

"Small but perfect. Douglas, Caelan and Izzadora."

"That's wonderful news, I'll tell all the boys," I said.

"Ian and I are going for a drink to wet the babies heads. Just wanted to say if anyone calls please feel free to offer them hospitality, there are plenty of bottles in the cupboard," Angus said.

"Thanks Angus but it's all quiet here. The four boys seem happy playing chess and I'm stitching. I'm not expecting anyone but thank you for the offer," I replied.

About 11:15pm the big brass door knocker shaped like a bridge sounded three times.

I opened the door to Percy and Iris, which came as a complete surprise. Percy, now in his 50's looked quite different when not in his chauffeur's uniform. He was wearing his best grey suit looking very dapper and pleased with himself. Iris looking radiant in black chiffon with a black beaded collar, wafted in on wave of 'Evening in Paris'.

"We've been for cocktails and dinner at the Metropole but saw the light on here and just had to call in to tell you our news!" Iris exclaimed, thrusting forward her left hand.

"You're engaged," was my rather startled response, as she'd only been widowed for a few months. "How wonderful."

"No point hanging about at our age," Percy said, gazing at his fiancée who was proudly showing us her neat sapphire and diamond three stone engagement ring.

"Congratulations" I said, hugging them both. "I've just heard Vera has had triplets, two boys and a girl."

"Never in the world," said Iris.

"Never in the world," repeated Percy.

"Would you like a drink, Angus said we could?" I offered.

They both agreed they would; then the door knocker sounded again.

Stan and Phyllis had reconciled, looking all loved up they announced that they would be getting married next year.

The third knock on the door brought Ada and Bertie into the party.

"He's pissed," said Ada. "I wouldn't offer him any more drink if I were you, he might throw up."

"Okay," I said. Thinking 'she's more than a little bit pissed herself.'

I noticed, sure enough, she was wearing the ring from Deveraux's window. Two diamonds, illusion setting, on a twist, so I assumed they were engaged.

I opened a bottle of champagne and poured everyone a glass, with lemonade for the four boys.

We drank a toast to Vera and the triplets. Then a toast to Iris and Percy. Then one to Ada and Bertie. Stan then bent down on one knee and proposed again to Phyllis who again said yes, so we drank another toast.

It's five minutes to midnight someone said, who will be the first foot.

We couldn't decide so, with no time to discuss the matter, all four boys decided to first foot together.

Stan gave them a shilling each. I ran to the kitchen to ensure they had salt and meantime they each collected a piece of coal from the scuttle.

As they went out into the front garden small flakes of snow were beginning to fall. The front door was closed.

Inside we listened for the park clock to chime midnight, which it soon did.

'Happy New Year' we all shouted as the boys came in together, snowflakes melting into their hair and on their pink cheeks.

We made a circle, crossed our arms and holding hands sang Auld Lang Syne.

It was Alfie who heard the telephone and shouted across to me, "It's the phone Bettina, it'll be Adam."

I flew into the study where there was a telephone extension and it was quieter.

"Happy New Year," Adam said.

"Oh Adam, it's been such a night. Vera has had triplets," I told him.

The connection was bad and the line crackled.

"Pikelets," he said. "What do you mean?"

"Not pikelets, TRIPLETS, Vera has had TRIPLETS," I shouted down the phone.

"My oh my, what an end to 1934," he said. "Is there a party going on?"

"Only a small one," I replied.

More crackling on the line.

"I thought I heard Adam telling me something about a friend called Larry but couldn't quite make out what he was saying on such a bad line.

The telephone became quiet again.

"Larry, Larry who?" I asked.

"Not Larry. I said marry. Will you marry me?"

"Yes of course I will," I answered, never having been more sure of anything in my life, "but when, how?"

"I'll be home in September next year – no this year now.

We'll have an engagement party, then make our plans."

'That seems a long way off', I thought, but said, "That will be wonderful Adam."

"I love you Bettina."

"I love you Adam. Happy New Y—"

The line went dead.

I rejoined the others in the hall where another bottle of champagne had been opened and a couple more logs placed on the fire.

"That was Adam, he wants us to get married when he comes home," I said, feeling a bit stunned.

They all cheered and shouted "A toast to Bettina and Adam."

The sing song lasted well into the early hours.

I've got you under my skin – duet sung by Ada and Bertie.

Cheek to cheek, Phyllis and Stan danced to demonstrate whilst we all sang.

Smoke get in your eyes – fortunately no one was smoking but Percy and Iris gazed into each other's eyes.

My two favourites were,

The Very Thought of You and *How deep is the Ocean*.

Pip just stretched out in front of the fire on the warm hearth rug, yawned, then fell asleep … as if to say,

"Enough excitement for one year. Happy 1935."

Little Bronze Girl

About the Author

Now enjoying retirement, Hettie lives in Buckinghamshire with her husband and two cats. Much of her time is devoted to her related passions of sewing, quilting and social history.

In her working years she developed an interest in the barriers women faced in all aspects of life, particularly related to health, family and work.

Hettie has been heartened to witness, in recent decades, the widening opportunities for women, although life/work balance continues to be tricky for most.

In her own career she has helped to support families as a nurse, midwife and health visitor.

Hettie's first book, *Threads of Steel* has now been expanded in this sequel, *Little Bronze Girl*.

The importance of female friendships and humour are illustrated throughout the story.

Finally, Hettie has appreciated the many kind comments from the readers of her first book and hopes that *Little Bronze Girl* brings pleasure and enjoyment to those who read it.